Walk Myself Home

WALK MYSELF HOME

An Anthology to End Violence Against Women

Edited by Andrea Routley

CAITLIN PRESS
HALFMOON BAY · BRITISH COLUMBIA

Caitlin Press Inc.
8100 Alderwood Road,
Halfmoon Bay, BC V0N 1Y1
www.caitlin-press.com

Text design by Rachel Page
Cover design by Pamela Cambiazo
Cover photographs by Tony Hoare

Printed in Canada

Caitlin Press Inc. acknowledges financial support from the Government of Canada through the Canada Book Fund and the Canada Council for the Arts, and from the Province of British Columbia through the British Columbia Arts Council and the Book Publisher's Tax Credit.

Canada Council Conseil des Arts
for the Arts du Canada

BRITISH COLUMBIA
ARTS COUNCIL
We acknowledge the support of the Province of British Columbia
through the British Columbia Arts Council

Library and Archives Canada Cataloguing in Publication

Walk myself home : an anthology to end violence against women / Andrea Routley.

ISBN 978-1-894759-51-9

1. Abused women—Literary collections. 2. Women—Crimes against—Literary collections. 3. Canadian literature (English)—Women authors. 4. Canadian literature (English)—21st century. I. Routley, Andrea, 1980-

PS8235.W7W34 2010   C810.8'03556   C2010-905735-X

Acknowledgements

I must thank my parents, Keith Routley and Geri Herron, whose support enabled me to complete this anthology. Thank you to Candace Fertile for her input and assistance during the editorial process. Finally, sincerest thanks to everyone who submitted writing, or who offered their encouragement and appreciation of this project. Your words have shaped this anthology.

CONTENTS

Andrea Routley

In order to end violence against women in our society, we must be able to recognize it, its perpetrators and when it happens—from the systemic forms to the extremes of direct violence to its subtler forms as put-downs or punch lines. Just as the persecution of a group does not occur without pre-existing prejudice, violence against women does not occur independently from a culture that condones attitudes of violence.

For many of us, the phrase "violence against women" conjures images of rape, influenced by film and television. We might imagine the cinematic version: a beautiful woman strides haphazardly down a potholed alleyway when she hears footsteps behind her. A quick glance over her shoulder, a flash of blond hair, and she increases her speed, but then, so do the footsteps. Her stride turns into a gallop until a heel gives way and she twists an ankle. She becomes a victim of monsters in dark alleys. Yet, that is hardly the scenario that most commonly happens; rape is more often perpetrated by a friend, an acquaintance, a relative or a partner.

How common is rape by a stranger? Years ago, on a hike, my sister and I were discussing the famous one-in-three statistic. A tree-planting co-worker enrolled in a women's studies program had said that one in three women experience sexual assault in their lifetime. I was skeptical.

"What do they consider assault?" I said. "Remember that guy Kendan?"

Kendan was a freeloading friend of a roommate's in Banff. One night after a show at the Rose and Crown pub, I walked home with him. We stopped briefly in front of some hotel where he planted a sloppy, drunken kiss on me, our tongues swirling like fish tails, then stumbled onward. When we got home, I gave him a blanket, said good night and started up the stairs to my room. Kendan grabbed my legs and the next thing I knew, his penis was inside me. I decided to relax until it was over, until he was finished, so it wouldn't hurt, then went to bed. The next day, he marvelled to our houseful of roommates that he had woken up with "no ginch." I was glad he didn't remember because I wanted to forget the whole thing.

"Those statistics probably count that as rape," I said to my sister, thinking one in three must be a gross exaggeration.

My sister paused a moment. "That's because that *is* rape."

I knew that what had happened was not consensual but until then, I had never identified the experience as "rape" because it was not how I understood it; Kendan was not a monster in a dark alley and I was not afraid of him.

I once saw a documentary about "corrective rape" in South Africa. Corrective rape is a current trend of punitive sexual violence against lesbians. In the film, one man says, "Once [a lesbian] gets raped by a guy, I think she'll want to know a way which is nice." It reminds me of a story I heard about "John," a tree planter, on the drive back to camp.

It was the end of the day and the conversation in the truck moved to gossip about other tree planters and crews, namely, a lesbian co-worker, whether she was really a lesbian and their theories as to why she had come out. Finally, one of John's co-workers concluded that she "just needed to get fucked" by John. If one substitutes the word "fucked" for "raped," the attitudes of the South African man in the documentary and that of the young Canadian tree planter are disturbingly similar.

Of course, "getting fucked" and "getting raped" are not the same thing; where "getting fucked" is supposed to be consensual, rape is not. However, in the tree planter's proposed scenario, does he imagine his lesbian co-worker would welcome "getting fucked" to become straight? She is not interested in men; the tree planter's proposal is an endorsement of sexual violence.

Though John didn't say anything at the time, this comment really bothered him; he recognized it as a form of violence against women. He told his foreman about it later.

As a lesbian, I've had this theory about "correcting" lesbianism with heterosexual sex told to me by complete strangers—once at a pub, once at a beach, once at a friend's party. Like John, I find myself tongue-tied in these moments, and the effects of these conversations are long-lasting; when my partner kisses me at a stoplight or takes my hand in public, I feel self-conscious, wondering if there is an onlooker considering how I might benefit from "getting fucked."

Women are taught to live defensively, and the culture of fear becomes second nature. It's part of our everyday lives. Several college online safety tips instruct students to "Walk midpoint between curbs and buildings, try to keep from using alleys or less-travelled routes between buildings, and avoid bushes."

When I read this I thought of "the monsters in dark alleys." Or even monsters that jump out of bushes. That is what we learn to fear. We're constantly being shown media images of women as victims. Prime-time TV depicts women being raped, stalked and murdered on a regular basis. A 2009 study from the Parents Television Council, titled *Women in Peril*, found a striking increase in the numbers of storylines and comedy punch lines that involved violence against women. The study found that depictions of violence against women, including beating, torture, rape, murder and threats, had increased 120 percent since 2004, while overall violence on television had increased 2 percent. (Depictions of teenage girls as victims had increased 400 percent.)

The change onscreen can distort our perceptions, and when violence against women appears commonplace, it becomes normal. A blatantly awful example of this was shown on an episode of *Two and a Half Men* (Season 6; Episode 16, aired March 2, 2009, on CBS), when one of the main characters, a young boy, takes pictures of himself with an unconscious, half-naked woman in his room, and there is canned laughter; this is supposed to be a joke. A half-hour later, a female murder victim is a plot device on a crime procedural show like *Law and Order* or *CSI*. These shows train us not to recognize the violence in our daily lives, yet consistently fear it.

I didn't recognize my own rape because Kendan did not "look like a rapist" to me. I thought, I must be misunderstanding or overreacting. I must be wrong. But when we doubt our own experiences, we lose our confidence and with that, the power to speak out. Perhaps if "John" had recognized the violence in his co-worker's comments right away, he might have found the words to speak out against such attitudes.

The following stories, poems and interviews reflect the variety of ways women experience violence. Whether it is physical abuse from a partner, sexual assault, a probing remark from a doctor or the graffiti in a workplace porta-potty, the writers speak from personal experience. These pieces are striking in the power and strength of character they reflect. Statistics can be overwhelming, yet do little to reveal the violence that surrounds us. By identifying violence against women in all its forms—from put-downs and inappropriate workplace humour to physical abuse—we will recognize it when it happens.

We would like to acknowledge that most of the contributors are from western Canada, specifically Vancouver Island. This is a result of the evolution of this project: *Walk Myself Home* began with the idea of creating a chapbook of local Victoria, BC, writers to be sold at the LoudSpeaker Festival the following year. As a result, the first calls for submissions were distributed locally. The project later expanded and the calls were sent to various organizations and networks throughout British Columbia and the Yukon. The final call for submissions was sent to national writers' associations, women's organizations and several universities. It was our intention to compile as diverse a collection of stories as possible. Of course, it is impossible to reflect all forms of experience, so we do not make the claim that this anthology fulfills such a task.

In addition to a call for written submissions, women and men were invited to share their stories, orally, in an interview. The purpose of these interviews was to include stories from women and men who may not be writers, but had the desire to share their experiences in this project. Individuals were invited through a general call, as well as individually by the interviewer, Emma Cochrane. All volunteers were consulted throughout the transcription process in order to ensure that what is published here reflects the details of their experiences and personalities to their satisfaction.

We have chosen not to organize this anthology by theme or forms of violence. Just as attitudes of violence are not separate from acts of violence, we did not want to imply a disconnection by organizing the narrative this way. Instead, pieces follow each other based on tone, perspective, subject and style to create a balanced rhythm.

I want to thank all the people who responded to the call for submissions, offered encouragement, ideas, assistance and writing. Regardless of whether your pieces were selected, you have informed those involved in the editorial process with your views and experiences.

To the reader, you have picked up this anthology for some reason. Perhaps you have experienced violence in your life and are seeking a book that reflects your experiences. Or perhaps someone you know has experienced gender-based violence. Maybe you are like so many who feel a frustration and anguish you cannot articulate, a persistent ache that tells you there is something wrong in our world, and are seeking the words, in poetry and prose, to express it. This anthology is for you.

Yvonne Blomer

VIOLENCE IS A BONE IN THE BODY

Metatarsal, Metacarpal, Maxilla,
Mandible. How violence bites.

It is a bone in the foot—Cuboid
It is a bone in the knee—Patella
It is a bone in the spine—Sacrum
In the torso—Xiphoid Process
In the shoulder—Fossa

In the brain, it is tissue.

It is in the cranial nerves,
it passes through Foramina (holes) in the skull.

It is a hair-line fracture.

MISOGYNY

During the seventeen years of the Vietnam War, it is estimated that fifty-eight thousand US service people died.

According to Men's Rape Prevention Project, Washington, DC, in that same seventeen-year period, fifty-one thousand women were killed, mostly by men they had close relationships with.

Rain fills the gutters; it shatters against panes like particles
of sorrow. This grief we carry, purple and heavy—

bent-limbed umbrella netting rather than repelling.
Men we have loved; women we have loved paired like tin

soldiers: against what we have hated; feared.
These abstracts: black bulbous; red seeping.

I want and I want and I want, wanting does naught.
I love and I love and I love, and then what?

Massacre of women and the murderer kills himself and we are left
looking to blame. It's too easy.

Crows wind-chase sparrow, clear the sky of that
near-geometric shape, leave a shattering of silence.

It seems we know war and death hold hands; but who and when—
well, right from the beginning love to violence:

that plastic groom on the wedding cake hides
his fist, or knife, his cock cocked, his bride

caught up, somehow, in the day and that lingering
doubt, only a shadow; some bird swift overhead.

We love it so much, we make more of it, colour our language
in this violence, so *everyday*: my son, deathly tired, and that's okay;

he died laughing; so stressed I could have killed—
and then somebody does and now language does and

the wind drives the rain, as if there is no stopping it.

I love and I hate and I want so, what so
just this morning, someone somewhere was raped.

She was killed by someone who *I do I do love you.*

Avra

ON KNOWING JEROME

Jerome never wanted me to have anything. I'd never seen anything like it.

He was always battering at me. "You stupid woman. You incompetent woman. You do everything appallingly."

Much later, an aquiline scowl: "What? I was only being funny."

Once he lay in my bed and told me I was worthless. "You have a bizarre sense of self-love," he would scold disapprovingly. But if you challenged his supremacy as a poet or as a performer, he would kill you.

Through a series of coincidences and upheavals, I moved into his flat. His lure was in his looks: all planes, height and darkness. Everything about him jutted—arrogant. His nose, his jaw, his sex. There was also the web of his voice and its utterances, spirals of zeniths and plunges, crafty rhythms, the stir of the skill.

I wanted to be a real performance poet, unmistakable, like he was. Except that he kept blocking my door to scoff, "You have no blinding poems," as I was on my way to a gig to perform. Once he lost control and said this in front of a guest. Mostly, though, his tormenting was kept hidden.

After a few weeks, I hid my prettiest things in a suitcase in the back of my closet. I knew he would try to destroy what was precious, what was beautiful. He wouldn't damage anything physically; he was too shrewd to leave a visible mark. But he would take away my pleasure, and leave my memories disfigured.

Before I moved in, I had only seen the outside, the poet. I didn't know the rhymes and rhythms masked a batterer. Once I became his lodger, I was isolated, trapped on the dingy fifth floor of a drug-ridden council estate. Banana peels and piss littered the elevator. The stairways were deserted and dangerous.

In seven months there, I never heard a laugh in the corridor: muffled curses and slammed doors were the currency of the building. I was usually exhausted by the time I reached our flat, and going back out seemed doubly exhausting— which left me inside with Jerome.

"Your best asset on stage is your voice," he declared imperiously. My voice? What about my writing skills or what I had to say?

"Fine. Would you rather I said your breasts? You have very lovely breasts and they look very nice onstage."

I remember thinking I was in bed with the devil. I suppose I looked frightened.

"Am I annihilating your ego yet?" he asked as I lay there, naked, and he attacked my personality.

"Why?" I grasped, through the fear, that he had revealed something important. "Have you done this before?"

A brief silence. "I don't know."

So he had done this before. Women had lain there, trying to love him, and he had casually, purposely destroyed them. I don't even know what else he said that morning. What I remember is the curt tone, the impenetrable indifference. I lay silent and then began to cry.

He barked, "Get up and go to work, you stupid woman."

This was the same man who'd said, "I think I'm in love with you," early on, when we'd only kissed, and he was still trying to get me to sleep with him. At that juncture, I was resistant, because I knew his sexual curiosity, fulfilled, would lead to nothing.

I see, in retrospect, my hesitation must have offended him. He cut off all contact, emotional and physical.

"It will never happen," he said of our mating. "The moment's passed." He said it as though he wasn't bothered. And he began to act as if I wasn't living in the house, as if my presence, when he noticed it, was a minor inconvenience.

This sudden and absolute removal of involvement, this disappearing of the person with whom you have been emotionally intimate, while they remain in front of you, can startle and frighten you in such a way that you fail to heal or recover. I read this and laugh, because on paper it looks melodramatic. But the assault of this vanishing was not melodramatic. It was the worst phenomenon I have ever experienced. So my understanding of it is hard-won.

I think of that famous poet, the one whose wives stuck their heads into ovens. He would never have had to lay a hand on them. Far from it. The opposite of involvement is what causes a fracturing of the psyche. It is the suggestion that your destruction will not matter.

He may have sat across the room, watching, as his wives pleaded with him to acknowledge them. The more they gesticulated, the more he would freeze, secretly enjoying their squirming humanity, congratulating himself for not need-ing to display such puerile emotion. More than any animated fury, his chosen indifference is what would have made the women hurl themselves into the heat, away from the frozen abyss that was their partner.

I understood the suicidal wives then—suddenly, viscerally. The rest, I could only see in hindsight. At the time, I was too panicked by his disappearance. And in a time-honoured pathology, I began trying to get him to sleep with me.

He wouldn't acknowledge our physical intimacy. I was just his "lodger," he told all and sundry, though he spent many nights in my room. He didn't care if this title humiliated me; he was unrepentant. He would come to my bed as long as I did not initiate physical contact. He'd lie there, sometimes with his arm around me. I think he wanted company.

After the decay of his last relationship, he couldn't manage anything but the most sporadic sex. His girlfriend had moved out in a rage, taking all the furniture. There was no TV or stereo to entertain him. Nothing in the house but the bookcases and me.

He was always mocking my desire, and expecting me to suffer for it. He'd push me off his lap and taunt me for being lustful. Or order me out of his bed, displaying shock at my presumption for entering his room, even after we'd spent hours kissing all over the house and even though we had already had sex a couple of times.

"You might get out of this situation when you move out of the flat," he said, in a tone encompassing both unconcern and smug pleasure. "Or you might not. You're just a woman with unfortunate taste in men." Once he said, "I'm crueller to you than to anyone else I like." He said it indifferently, as if he were observing the colour of ants.

Why did I stay? I had learned to cherish his voice and his face onstage, before I knew what rotted behind them. And despite his outbursts of evil, I sensed love under the hate. He would show it sometimes. He'd spend hours talking to me and remember even the smallest details of what I told him. So I trusted my instincts—that he loved me, that this bizarre hostility couldn't last forever, that love must win out in the end.

"You long-suffering woman," he'd say in an amused tone. "You long-suffering woman." Once he put his hand on my shoulder and told me, "The hard, brutal truth is I've never really fancied you." I walked out. He followed. "I've always fancied you," he said.

I remember this particularly, as the best example of the many times he changed tone and opinion in the space of three minutes. I was sharing a flat with a slew of personalities in the body of one big sadist. And none of them were on speaking terms.

"I fancy you entirely," he announced drunkenly. "That's part of the problem. What I mean is I've never really wanted to go out with you." I knew it was fruitless to remind him of when he'd thought differently, since he had no recognition of what he'd said or done even moments before.

Eventually, I learned to speak to him very calmly. The use of a flat, emotionless tone enabled him to hear things, whereas my anger was only ever met with colossal returns of rage. So I spoke quietly and patiently, as to a child.

"Do you want me to hate you?" I would ask, pausing to explain in an understanding voice, "If you keep acting this way, I'm going to hate you."

"No! I don't want you to hate me. I don't want anyone to hate me!" Then, begrudgingly, almost sullenly, "I especially don't want you to hate me."

Throughout those seven months, I could feel myself disintegrating. On most days, I felt hatred being burned into me and I knew the damage would be cumulative and irreparable. Walking into the house meant walking into a seething pit of rage; he was always there, always home, alone, waiting.

No one seemed to understand the gravity of what was happening. I had no money with which to move out—my rent was only thirty-five pounds a week—and it was a freezing winter, which paralyzed me. Landlords wanted security deposits. You may wonder how I could let something like that stop me when I needed to save myself, but the days of nightmares were punctuated with periods of normalcy, when he would speak to me lovingly or laugh with me and tell me I was family.

Also, I was so emotionally spent I almost didn't want to leave. I wanted to stay until it could be fixed. I still couldn't fathom the levels of hate and hostility that oozed out of him and onto me every time I entered the house. I kept waiting to make sense of what was happening.

But there was no plausible explanation. And then: two months after I moved out, we started going out. One evening I stopped by, at his request, and brought along a letter delineating precisely what he'd done to my spirit and state of mind. His more sentient self responded—I don't know why; maybe it was its turn to mind the fort—and suddenly we were a couple. He took me to bed, kissing me for hours before we even undressed, touching me so lovingly and gently I wondered why he hadn't always done this.

I went out with him out of relief—so people would know I hadn't imagined the connection between us, which he'd always publicly denied. So they'd know I wasn't making it all up. So I could confirm to myself that I wasn't wrong in my impression of what had gone on—in the intensity of our connection. And of course, so I could experience the love that always seemed to be sitting there, somehow immobile or immobilized, waiting for me under the hatred.

When we went out, he gave me nothing. He would lull me into a state of vulnerability by acting normal, loving, and then he would attack. Poets wound with words and he was doing all he could to scar me. He must have known he was a monster. But he thought it was my problem, because he didn't need me.

After a summer of elaborate sex and more elaborate arguments, he broke up with me. Over poetry. I said something that revealed him in public as poetically egotistical.

"You should shut your fucking gob," he said. "You should really shut your fucking gob sometimes."

"Are you practising to be a wife beater?" I asked, and left before he actually considered trying to hit me. He'd taken to slapping my sides in an unpleasant manner and once goaded me, "You've never been hit. You don't know what it means to be hit." He seemed displeased that I'd never suffered the experience. He seemed to think I'd never suffered enough in general. "You're used to people liking you," he said, in a tone of disapproval.

There's one thing that may be hard to understand. I still wasn't ready to give him up. I felt that only he could heal what he'd destroyed for me. Also, I couldn't shake the impression there was someone normal in there, trapped and frightened, jailed in a body and a mouth directed by a psychotic prison warden.

This might seem like an elaborate weaving of excuses, but it was always what I perceived. Sometimes I imagined him as a roulette wheel—six personalities: five horrible, one nice, and you never knew which was going to spin up to top position and be in control . . . for the instant. My problem was I loved the one kind personality. I loved talking to it and I kept waiting for it to reappear.

When we broke up, I called, overcome with grief that all the poets we knew seemed to think he'd never liked me and he was allowing them to think that. "Why don't you just tell them you liked me?" I asked. "Please."

I wanted him to protect me for once, to be a little bit manly. "As if I'd ever have the chance to work that into a conversation," he scowled. A part of me watched, amazed, as he let me sob hysterically, in a crumpled ball, in lieu of his having to announce, "I liked her." A person I had spent so many nights and days with, who had told me, "Things aren't always easy with you, but when it is easy, it's sensational." But me holding out the words as proof is nothing. Besides, there are very few words to show. He always avoided the words.

Two months later, we were in bed again. I unfailingly resorted to the bedroom as a place to wring intimacies out of him. "You have a disease," he explained in a rare moment of gentleness. "And it's me."

His amusement was unseemly and, like everything else about him, cruel. My unshakeable desire for closeness with him embarrassed me. I felt lumbered with a bodily function I couldn't control, and I needed him to be gentlemanly and never mention it.

Instead, he seemed to mention nothing else.

I'm not going to put a pretty ending on this. Jerome moved out of London but the damage he inflicted remained for years. It took years to feel light again, free again, me again. Before, I'd never grasped that emotional abuse alone could wreak physical damage, but it can. I didn't have to cut myself or hurt myself for this to happen; it was enough that my heart so often pounded from uncertainty and fear, that my moods would plunge and my stasis and equilibrium were constantly overturned. By the time we separated, my insides were wrecked. It took years of love, serene surroundings, meditation and prayer to clean them out.

There's nothing poetic about female fear—and that's what it all adds up to in the end.

Rhona McAdam

SPRING CLEANING

I've hung the shirt you left
head down on the line,
wheeled it to the end of the garden
where spiders spin ligatures
between your arms.

Hung it out to dry
where flies settle
their changing minds, and wasps
forage without mercy
for the sweetness
that rots around you.

I'll see you in tatters,
battered shapeless by a wind
that is gentle one day,
hurricane the next,
till there are no arms
left to raise and the neck
is empty of shouting.

I plan to leave it there
till the sky burrows
through your heart, and rain
shimmies down the weft,
feeds the grass
with what's left of you.
And I can root myself in that.

In the end when you're small
enough to disappear
I'll scatter you like
ash, a bit of nothing
for strangers to brush away.

Janet Baker

LES

I don't remember my one and only figure-skating solo
there at the Winnipeg Winter Club,
only those moments just before, me
at the boards waiting for the music, knowing I was in way over my head,
that my pathetic attempt at a "program" could only be an embarrassment.

I don't remember the music, imagine it was soaring, and sublimely orchestral,
don't remember it at all, how it went, how it ended, whether I managed
a spin, a camel, perhaps a three-jump, whether there was even a ripple
of polite applause. I could do my figure eights, was never good at anything else
but if you took lessons, you eventually had to do a solo. And I don't remember

my role as a king in an operetta called The Magic Fishbone, but I have evidence,
a black and white photograph of the cast, me in my kingly regalia, behind us
our shadows, amorphous, hovering, and I have no recall
of my costume or its colour, probably a very royal maroon, and the stockings are definitely
white, and who knows why I was playing the king

in an obscure story by Charles Dickens at 7:30 p.m. that December 9th and 10th
and the program doesn't give the year so I don't know how old I was but I'd guess around
eleven, maybe around the same time I was taking those figure-skating lessons, maybe even
around that time that Les drove me home, maybe he was driving me home from a rehearsal,
because it was a junior choir production and his daughter's in the picture too,

but then, why wasn't she in the car, why just me and Les? And I'm thinking now of my recurring
dream, the one where I'm in a play and I've lost my script and I can't seem to borrow one and I
haven't learned my lines, and then I'm on stage, the curtains swinging open and I'm out there
exposed and this is where the dream always gets blurry. And maybe the dream is connected to
this photo, the role I can't remember, and maybe

if I could dream about being in the car with Les I might remember why
he was driving me home, what happened, after he told me
I was old enough, after he told me he would give me a thrill, his hand
reaching across the front seat towards my thigh, might remember going home,
remember something besides a street light and that it was near the tracks.

Kelly Pitman

QUIET LITTLE GIRLS

How old was I, the first time a man put his hands on me? I was standing on an escalator, feet beside my mother's, my canvas sneakers an echo of hers. Eight, maybe, or nine? We were at the Bay, heading for the cafeteria for hamburgers, fries and milkshakes. It must have been a Saturday for my mother to have had time. I had half-noticed a grizzled sort of man getting onto the escalator after us, but I could not have described his face or his clothing. He slid his hand between my legs and pushed at me through my pants. I stood motionless, barely breathing. Like someone who has just been told there is a snake beneath her chair, I was paralyzed, waiting for it to be over. Then we reached the next floor and walked away. The hand stayed behind.

Why wouldn't I cry out? There was no inner debate—it never occurred to me to protest. I was a shy kid, always tending to bear whatever pain or humiliation the world served up, for I had learned somehow, and perhaps erroneously, that protest only prolongs torture. Silence was no weapon but it was a refuge. Whatever gasp welled up in my lungs, I held it there. My breath, my face, at least, I could control. But I suspect that even a noisier, more confident girl would not have cried out at that moment, something like shame stopping her throat as easily as it stopped mine.

Silence was not then and is not now a protection from memory, however. I can still see the iron steps disappearing into the floor above. I can still feel the probing fingers. I can still sense the moment unwinding, though the hours before and after are as lost to me as if they'd never happened, or as if they were trapped in the quiet chamber of someone else's skull.

But then that is how memory works. Childhood becomes a series of poses and gestures and words, fragments cut off from their befores and afters.

Like statues, the game we played in backyards and which children may play still. Sometimes, we would clasp hands and whirl around, then let go suddenly, flinging each other across the grass, and when we stopped—sitting, standing, crouched, splayed—we had to freeze until we were released by a voice. Sometimes a whirler would spin two or three others at once, the group of us like a soft propeller suddenly breaking into pieces. Other times, we'd all dance wildly about until the controller called, "Statues," and we'd have to stop exactly as we were. Last one to move wins.

I remember playing this game at the Krugers' house, which was across the alley from ours, with my brothers and the two granddaughters of the Krugers. Mr. and Mrs. Kruger were an elderly couple who looked after my youngest brother, the only one of us not yet in school. There was no daycare in those days, and our family was the only single-parent family in the neighbourhood (or in the world, so far as I knew). My mother left early and came home late, walking to and from work to save the bus fare, and we fended for ourselves more than other children did. For a little while, my grandmother lived with us, but she moved downtown, and while other children came home to peanut-butter sandwiches and glasses of milk set out on sunlit tables (or so I imagined it), we came home to forage in the fridge or among the shelves in the hall by the back door. Mrs. Kruger, for a short time, must have set out sandwiches and milk for my brother. And even when he was older and trusted to tumble about with the rest of us, we would sometimes— especially when the Kruger girls were visiting—play in the Krugers' backyard, so carefully tended compared to our clover-strewn patch of earth.

One of the girls, Elizabeth, was deaf. Her deafness was never explained to me and it never occurred to me to ask why she couldn't hear. When people mentioned it, they'd always say things like, "You'd never know it to look at her," as if deafness should show on the face, should mark her grotesquely, and this made her beauty more apparent even to me, though children tend to find beauty where they love rather than to love where they see beauty. She *was* beautiful though, long-limbed, graceful, smooth-skinned, with green-flecked grey eyes and waving honey-coloured hair. I knew that she was far more beautiful than I. Although I did not yet, as I would soon, see only my ugliness when I looked at my reflection. I did not yet, as I would soon, avoid my reflection whenever possible.

More than her beauty, I loved her silence. Hers seemed an ideal version of my own. Like me, she almost never spoke, but unlike me, her silence was not a failure or a worry, but natural, defensible. Her silence was merely the extension of her strange loveliness. More than that, she accepted my quietness. With her, I need not speak, for she could not hear me, and yet I often felt a deep communion with her, as if we had spoken of our truest perceptions and found them the same.

Her grandfather, Mr. Kruger, was a big, balding, jocund man with a voice like a truck. Like most children, I tended to move through rooms of adults like a gopher across an open field. I never knew when someone might boom out a question at me, forcing me to mumble some response, then mocking or chiding my too-hushed, too-slight answer. Mr. Kruger particularly made me cringe, for he was loudly jovial, hearty of body and voice, an almost comical contrast to his wife, who was a twittering songbird in an apron.

And here is another one of those moments. In the living room, Mr. Kruger insists that I sit on his lap, and there I am, trying to please but awkward and mute, bony legs dangling and hands fisted in my lap. Then his hand is under me, then it is between my legs, then it is sliding inside my shorts, then his wife bustles in, then I am somehow free, my feet back on the ground and headed for the door, my legs shuddering. But before I am free, somewhere between his urgent and obscenely cheerful violation and the appearance of Mrs. Kruger, my eyes meet Elizabeth's, and there passes between us a look more quietly full than any of our other communication.

That year, the Krugers dropped by near Christmas, as people do, bringing cookies and exclamations about the weather. My brothers and I darted in and out of rooms. With Christmas only days away, we had a childish impatience with adult talk. Another moment: the Krugers stand at the back door, on their way out. Mr. Kruger looms even larger in his woollen coat and rough toque, and he is holding his arms wide, his thick-jointed fingers big and meaty in the pale winter light. Voices are urging me to step across the safety of the kitchen, past the heavy table and the empty coffee cups and the plates of cinnamon buns and cookies, past the bowls of oranges and nuts that my mother has paid for with hard work and that we have paid for by going without her every day and learning to protect ourselves.

"Go on, don't be shy, give Mr. Kruger a hug." And for once, I am brave. I hang my head, but silence is a kind of strength at last, and after a while, they resort to talking about me instead of to me. Then they give up, and they go.

And what about Elizabeth? If I saw her again, I don't remember it, and I cannot say whether that is because design or caution kept me from the Krugers' house or because I have forgotten everything about her from the day I sat on her grandfather's lap.

I have three pictures of her in my head, and only in one is she frozen. I see her sitting cross-legged on the lawn, listening with her eyes, her hands singing in the air to mirror mine as I explain with gestures how to play the game. I see her at the moment before she lets go of my hands, our long hair flying, the shape of us like a butterfly on the dappled grass. And I see her still as stone, her eyes speaking to me across her grandparents' living room, telling me what she could not tell me any other way, perhaps what she could not tell anyone else, and hasn't still.

Fiona Tinwei Lam

CAMOUFLAGE

Outside, pacing fury:
a plywood door
prepares to buckle.

Inside, a legless bed floats
docked against a wall.

Medusas in the wallpaper's
clumped foliage peer
into an empty shag sea.

A narrow closet,
innards jumbled—
woolly hems, boots and
a twelve-year-old.

Her crouched silence.
She pretends to be
a shoe.

"Camouflage" was first published in Intimate Distances *(Nightwood Editions)*

Janet K. Smith

THE AUDITION

Amanda takes a deep breath, tightens her stomach muscles for balance and lifts up, onto her toes. She sweeps her arms upwards, then out and down, to form a perfect circle. At twelve, her young muscles easily hold her steady while she twists her head in an attempt to see more of herself in the bedroom mirror. She'd watched *The Nutcracker* suite on TV last week and was excited to see kids her own age floating across the stage in their costumes. She looks at herself in the mirror again and pulls her shoulders back and down. She looks good. There's an audition for the after-school dance club on Wednesday next week and it's all she can think about.

When the front door slams, she slumps onto her heels. She needs to convince her parents that dance won't interfere with her chores, but it's already after five. Heavy footsteps come closer, and her bedroom door flies open.

"What are you doing? Where's your mother?" He moves off before she can answer, leaving behind air that swirls with criticism and annoyance. It fills her room, forcing her out.

She heads straight out to the woodshed, hoping he won't notice the bin is still empty. She shouldn't have left this chore so late but it's a dirty job and she always seems to pick the wrong logs. Pulling her wheelbarrow alongside the stack, she grabs the dry, cedar logs from one end of the pile. They drop into the metal base with a satisfying *thump*. Puffs of dust mushroom up around her, filling her mouth and nose with the musty, grainy tang of drying wood. Thankful for her gloves, she wipes the cobwebs, pillbugs and clumps of soil from each piece, and carefully positions them for the bumpy journey across the lawn.

Reaching the house with her load intact, she opens the little square door on the outside of the house to reveal the small compartment for storing firewood. Amanda starts unloading the wheelbarrow and flings the first piece of wood up and inside the bin; it thumps hard against the little door below that opens to the living room. Almost before it can drop to the base of the bin, her father pulls open the door below and grabs the offending piece of wood. His thick, strong fingers slam the chunk tight against the wall of the wood bin. Amanda freezes as his arm reaches up, yanks the next piece out of her hands, and crams it tight beside the first one. The clunk of wood on wood jolts her back in motion and she works faster, trying hard to stack the wood pieces in a straight row, as his moccasins point at her from the other side.

Just as she's done loading the wood, he wrenches the biggest piece of wood from the centre of the stack. "It would be nice if just once I could make a fire without having to deal with these oversized chunks, but it's all about making it easy for Amanda, isn't it?" he says. She's still outside the open chute when she hears her father start to chop the wood into kindling. *Lazy, stupid, selfish, foolish.* Every swing of his hatchet cuts away at her.

She slowly returns the wheelbarrow to the woodshed, her steps heavy with his disapproval. She tilts the wheelbarrow against the side of the outbuilding, steps back and takes a deep breath. With the wood bin done, her mind opens to her surroundings and she hears a pair of robins gossiping in the fir tree beside her. She likes it back here, away from the house. Music from *The Nutcracker* runs through her head and the yard transforms into a stage. She is the Sugar Plum Fairy with gossamer wings. Her gumboots take little hopping steps, landing softly on the layers of needles and moss as she moves through the trees. With a quick left-legged jump, she kicks her right leg high to the sky. Her gumboot sails off her foot, hits a branch and lands a few feet in front of her, covered in needles and twigs from its collision with the fir tree. Careful to keep her exposed sock away from the wet, muddy ground, she hops to her fallen boot and slips it back on. She giggles to herself and runs toward the grassy area behind the house, happy to be rid of her nastiest chore. Prancing by the patio doors, she glances inside and sees her father sitting in his La-Z-Boy with his usual scotch and water. Their eyes lock. She stops dancing.

It's time to set the table. She dreads the silent storm that accompanies each family meal. *Maybe they'll be happy if I set the perfect table. I can't put out everything from the fridge, but I can't miss anything either.* She decides on ketchup, milk, butter and dressing. She chooses placemats, counts out cutlery and carefully reaches for the plates and drinking glasses. With the table set, she returns to the kitchen where she risks a quick pirouette. She stumbles and tries again. While Amanda is mid-twirl, her mother walks in, arms loaded with groceries and followed by two fussing toddlers. An exasperated look from her mother drops Amanda back onto her heels. She hangs her head. *Stupid, thoughtless girl. Why was I dancing when there's so much to do?*

"I see your father's home. Stop flitting around and make yourself useful. Here." She pushes the paper bags into Amanda's chest. "Put these away. I've got to feed these kids." Her mother yanks open the fridge and pulls out some carrots.

The air grows tense.

"Where's the bloody ketchup? Don't tell me we're out. These kids won't eat anything without ketchup on it."

Rushing to grab the ketchup off the dining room table, Amanda's hand knocks a glass and watches in horror as it smashes on the floor.

"Jesus Christ. Don't I have enough to do? Get the dustpan, and help clean this up before the kids get hurt."

Amanda's father appears. He's on his way to the kitchen for another drink. They stand to let him pass. He strolls through the commotion, rolling his eyes at their efforts to clean up. Amanda feels the chaos magnify and she glances at her mother to see how much trouble she's in. Her heart sinks as she sees anger and frustration on her mother's face. *Now Mom's mad and Dad's fed up and it's all my fault. Why can't I do things right?*

Her mother heads to the kitchen and Amanda can hear her bemoaning the need to make separate meals for everyone. Pots and utensils are yanked out and slammed on the counter as her mother darts from the cupboard to the fridge, then the sink, the stove and back again. She drops a lid and it rattles and spins as it hits the floor. Amanda tries to help but she's distracted by the noise. *Will it bring him back to the kitchen?*

"What's the matter with you? Get out of the way," her mother barks as she rushes to finish cooking.

By 6:45, dinner is on the table and Amanda relaxes when her father smiles at his steak and potatoes. The toddlers use their hands to grab their ham and cheese bits, while she and her mother eat their beans and toast.

"Did you get any wine?" her father asks.

Amanda's mother jerks back her chair, almost tipping it over as she races to get the wine for him. She barely sits back down when he holds up the salt and wags it at her. She goes to the kitchen to refill the shaker.

"I don't see any HP Sauce," he says as she sits again.

Amanda's mother is half out of her seat before he grabs her arm and tells her to sit down. He points to his daughter. "She can get it. The table's her job."

Amanda pushes back her chair, and reminds herself, *don't run*. She retrieves the bottle as quickly as she can. "Here, Dad. Sorry. I'll remember next time." Amanda makes a mental note to add HP to the must-have list, and watches him pour himself more wine.

Four drinks down, she counts silently. Her father suddenly puts down his fork and looks at her. He's smiling. "I saw the neatest trick today," he says. "This guy was able to keep a metallic ribbon up in the air using this special wand. The ribbon floated like magic."

"That's a levitation rod! I saw one on the Internet and we learned in school that it uses static electricity to keep the ball in the air. We didn't have a rod but we did the exact same thing with balloons—"

"If you were playing with balloons, then it's not the same thing now, is it?" he cuts her off. "Do you even know what static electricity is? How does the electron interact? What do the nuclei do?" She doesn't know and goes quiet. With dinner over, he pushes back his chair, refills his glass with wine and heads toward his La-Z-Boy.

The phone rings just as Amanda and her mother finish cleaning the kitchen. Amanda answers and her face brightens. "It's Jen," she mouths to her mother. Her mother smiles and leaves her alone. Amanda lifts her left heel onto the side board, stretches her right arm over her head and bends to touch her toes as she talks about boys, homework and the dance club. Jen is telling her about a sign-up sheet when she hears a *click* in her ear and the phone goes dead. Puzzled, she straightens and drops her leg to the floor. She turns to see her father with his hand on the disconnect button.

"Ten minutes is up," he says and walks away. Amanda flushes with embarrassment as the phone rings again.

"I can't talk anymore. I've got to go," she whispers and hangs up. She sits alone in the kitchen for a few minutes then, hearing the theme song from her favourite TV show, she heads to the living room to watch. She decides today's not the best day to mention the dance club and stays quiet to keep the peace.

At 9:00 p.m. she gives the expected good-night kiss to each parent and heads to bed. Safely in her room, she closes her eyes and carefully balances up onto her toes. Her arms sweep upward, then out and down, as they form a perfect circle. She climbs into bed and hugs her pillow as she whispers a prayer. "Please God, help me be a better daughter. I promise to try harder. Just please let them see, let them understand that I need to join the dance club. I promise to be perfect. Just please let me join. Amen."

Sheila Martindale

AT THE NURSING HOME

We look
not at each other
but out over the garden—
roses and rhododendrons
lush green lawn
the incessant English drizzle

From time to time
we glance
each other's way
nervously
thinking of what to say

You remark on my greying hair
with a hint of satisfaction
as if middle age
were yet another of my failings

I note the cane held
in your trembling hand
at one time
it might have been a weapon
I feel again the crack of ribs
the fierce rush of pain
the gush of bloodstained vomit

You are small now
your belligerence shrunk
to this flicker of old hostility

You complain about the food
the lack of care
the infrequence of my visits

We stare at rain
streaking the window
like remembered tears

Jancis M. Andrews

FAMILY VIEWING: FATHER

And sometimes he would torture our dog, clamping
Tecky's muzzle in his big hand, twisting
until Tecky's head was upside-down
like a black mass, the dog moaning
prayers through its teeth, my sister and I
screaming alongside, his other big hand
holding us off, his giggling crackling
around the room, his eyes coals
beneath charcoal hair, our tears burning
in his smoking breath.

His fingers were brands
on my breasts,
my developing body.
These, and other assaults
we never forgave.
When he died, only then
did we believe in a merciful God
who answered prayers.

He never spoke of his childhood.
For us, he was only the Great Fire
consuming his daughters
for twenty-six years. His name
was Tom: our synonym
for hate.

Years after his death, Mother told me
his red-headed father never called him
by name, only "black bastard"
because of his black hair, and that
when Tom was five, Grandfather rose

from the farm table and silently
flung him into the big kitchen fire,
held up the blazer, and up Tom roared.

It took six men
to pull Grandfather off. A miracle
you didn't die, they said
when they pulled Tom out, flesh melting
living torch
in his father's auto-da-fé.

And now I know he never left
that place, and that his soul
revolved endlessly about a stake,
finding no way out through those grown-up faces
and that he never stopped shrieking
his aloneness in those flames,
so he tried to pull
        his daughters in.

And now at last I can call you
by your name, oh my father, and let go
my own burning.
When old hatreds kindle,
I shall stand beside you
in your father's fire, hand in hand,
our flesh unravelling, eyes bubbling
in our heads, till our streaming tears
put out our mutual hell.

"Family Viewing: Father" appeared in Canadian Woman Studies, *Summer 1991, Vol. 2, No. 4*

FAMILY VIEWING: MOTHER

Even in her coffin
Mother's face was clenched, as if
she could not let go
while there was yet another bill to pay,
as usual, on the never-never.
What did you do, Mother,
when Saint Peter clocked you in?
Did you automatically lift
your pail and brush, begin to scrub
at those pearly gates?
Ah, my mother, my lady
most immaculate, you always had
a double shift: housewife
and cleaning lady, while Dad,
aping all government,
docked a dollar from your housekeeping
for every dollar earned.

So your frown, Mother,
was that a message that Heaven, too,
is just another kind of never-never,
that even in death there is no rest?
Or was that face a message
for my father, telling him you had
nothing left to give,
only your face
clenched like a fist?

"Family Viewing: Mother" appeared in BOA, *No. 2, Summer 1988*

Fazeela Jiwa

CLEANUP TIME

Youngest:

When she was youngest, Amara obeyed. Obeyed: folded socks and waxed furniture upon the mother's request. Obeyed: wiped the curry-splattered table nightly with the mother's smelly two-year-old J-Cloth. Good as new after a run through the dishwasher, the mother insisted.

It smelled like the last two years were trapped inside and rotting.

The mother's rules, strictly timed: morning cleanup time involved detailing the bathroom sink with her fingernails while she brushed her teeth, wiping the toilet trunk as she urinated, scrubbing the tub during her shower. She poured Amara's cereal, and to the sound of crunching Amara watched. Counters, cupboards, coffee pot. Fridge, faucets, freezer.

Midday cleanup time varied depending on the day, from reorganizing photo albums to vacuuming the ceiling. Evening cleanup time included Amara. She was charged with setting and cleaning the table, and placing the dishes in the dishwasher, after the mother had washed them in the sink. Rules were comfortable. They were not even rules, because Amara had not yet conceived of dissent.

Amara learned English through mimicking incoherent sounds on TV and at school. She taught the mother a song:

Clean up, clean up, everybody, everywhere,
Clean up, clean up, everybody do your share.

Top-lung singing made the J-Cloth less odorous; it made cleanup time exciting, even if Amara did not fully understand the words she shoutsang. If she did, she would have found them contradictory, because it was not everybody, everywhere who cleaned up. It was only the mother and Amara when she helped. The father and the baby brother lounged and burped and occasionally laughed at her song with the English sounds. When Amara did not help, the mother cleaned up alone, in the silent stench of dinners past, festering within the fibres of the J-Cloth.

Amara's father had "a temper."

Confusing. Why didn't the mother say he had a *bad* temper? Everyone has *a* temper, but the absence of "bad" or "good" deprived Amara of a sense of the mother's moral compass. But Amara suspected that probably this type of temper was bad.

Mostly he came home late, but on some days he came home right after work, so Amara and the mother reheated the dinner every hour to ensure its temperature whenever he came. If he found dinner cold or undesirable, he would have "a temper." Loud, broken English gleaned from the taxi trade, more words Amara mimicked without understanding: "Fock, beech, I work fockin har in fockin hale for u-beech." The father pounded the table and slammed the door, and squealing tires sped him away to Kentucky Fried Chicken to purchase a better dinner from a cute blond girl. He ate downstairs, alone. He left greasy garbage and chicken bones for the mother to clean up, evidence that fried chicken trumped curry.

Secretly, Amara envied the father. Her jowls slackened for Kentucky Fried Chicken. Amara helped clear the dinner-now-relegated-to-tomorrow's-lunch until the mother's eyes glossed and Amara knew she was lost in cleanup time. Then she snuck downstairs to beg a fried chicken breast from the father. The father spoiled Amara and she loved him guiltily. Daddy's Little Girl, he said. How come he was not this nice to the mother? How come he did not share his chicken with her? She was the leftover chicken grease staining the couch or the paper bucket the better dinner came in: Translucent. Ghostly. And the bucket of fried chicken was the father's heart: he could only share one piece. Amara gobbled the whole thing herself, offering none to the mother.

Guilty.

But so sick of curry.

Younger:

When she was younger, Amara destroyed. Angrily. Purposefully. There lay the world to explore, why must she clean her room? Who gave a fock if she folded her socks or waxed her furniture?

Amara resented the mother's rules. Her stupid cleanup time song. Her habits. Especially the ones that Amara learned to adopt, like bowing her head passively to defer confrontation. At school, she could talk like them; she collected English words to best them at their own language. But they still won, because some words came out wrong. It didn't matter that she memorized *Of Mice and Men*, because she said *Gee-or-gee* instead of *Jorj*. Those mistakes belonged to the mother because she told Amara to say it that way. When the class mimicked her misplaced accent in great peals of laughter, she defended herself the way the mother did: silently bowing her head, scrunching up until the confrontation ended, then scrubbing the floor. Suds masked her tears that broke the oily soap rainbows.

A stark difference slowly wedged between Amara and the mother. When Amara bowed her head, she hid her eyes slit in rage. Her silence curbed the cursing she learned from the father. Anger, resentment, violence bubbled in her.

Amara saw the power that the father enjoyed. His voice boomed so loud, it hardly mattered if his words came out accented. The mother suggested a new word to impress them next time, but the father suggested "beating the *sheet* from them." That sounded much more satisfying, especially considering the mother's protest, a horrified eyebrow, slightly raised before obediently fetching tea.

No rules applied to the father. He made them up, different every day. He overturned the mother's rules without explanation. After months of earnestly convincing the mother of the merits of *Seventeen* Magazine, Amara proudly produced it from her backpack for the drive home from mosque. She fought her brother for the front seat because she wanted her hair to blow in the wind as she read her magazine, arm hung nonchalantly out the window except to sexily pull back the hair from her mouth. The father abruptly decapitated this daydream image of herself; he grabbed the magazine and threw it out the window, swearing loudly about today's girls. With the repressed outrage of a second-generation teen raised Muslim, Amara wailed until she was told to "Shetap!" then whirled to face the mother in burning indignation. The mother bowed her head, organized her purse.

He made the mother's rules impotent. Weak. He showed Amara: all it took was will. A loud voice. "A temper."

Despite this new-found condescension for weakness, Amara raged the most at the mother's deference to the father. She had so easily learned the secret power of simply breaking the rules. Why couldn't the mother? So easy just to swear back, leave, destroy everything. Instead, the mother sniffled to the sound of Swiffer. She always got in the way. Four-foot-eleven and barely audible, her words trapped in the space between transmission and reception. Only her lost eyes suggested bigness. Amara grew larger than her.

Destruction reigned in the mother's clean house. No, *the father's* clean house. The house was his, but the cleanliness was hers. The furniture was his, that solid, necessary, adult stuff. Bureaus and bedside tables. But the stuff was hers. Stuff: that amorphous collection of the professional consumer, those empty folks cramming junk that never alleviates the insatiable well of need. Foot spas, old mops, Swiffer refill packages, broken umbrellas, rusty exercise equipment, assorted cleaning solutions, old furniture wax, smelly sale candles.

The mother: a pack-rat neat-freak. Everything the mother once needed lay compartmentalized in the porcelain dollhouse that she never left. "Since you never leave, why do you keep all that shit?" Amara asked in perfect English, pointedly and cruelly. The mother saved her everything for Amara, so she could have it and the mother could not. So the mother could sacrifice. Mother martyrdom.

The mother gave everything, everything of herself. The first bite of each meal, her nicest earrings. Her labour for homework.

Her dignity to keep the peace.

Amara recoiled from the sacrifices, which were not really sacrificial but they would be taken anyway. Sacrifice, slaughter—semantics enabled the mother to cope with her oppression. Amara didn't even want what the mother gave. She had her own Kentucky Fried food; she had her own plastictacky jewellery. Amara did her own homework and didn't trust the mother's immigrant version of knowledge anyway. She did not want the frayed J-Cloths of two years prior that washed with the dishes of dinners rejected, soaked with the mother's silent tears.

Amara wanted the mother to rage back at the father.

The father's most recent defiance dented Amara's admiration for him. The mother had shown Amara perfumed letters signed with a lipsticked kiss mark called "Katrina." Katrina dotted her i with a heart. Amara immediately stopped wearing perfume and lipstick. She stopped dotting her i's with hearts. The father's rebellion that she had so admired suddenly turned against her. She had no one to admire now. Pity for the mother, anger for the father. She was outraged. Stung.

But the mother, her shoulders just hunched a little bit more, unsurprised. This new knowledge would not change her life; it would go on like before but with a little bit more humiliation.

Amara's feeling of betrayal singed with secret empathy for the father. She wondered about Katrina, the blond, blue-eyed, Kentucky Fried employee.

Midday sun blared into the kitchen windows. The heat roared like loud, inescapable orders. Oppressive. Amara watched the mother warm rejected dinner for lunch in the microwave, emotional leftovers.

Young:
When she was young, Amara repented. Immense guilt trapped her at home; the burden of the sole joy bringer. She attempted a return to the helpful child she had once been but all the stresses of a second parent pressed upon her. Amara dreamed of escape.

Perhaps if she tidied the house and her appearance, goodchildthings, Amara could feel less guilty about learning life, leaving the mother, home, alone, chained by the nuclear family and four televisions. Amara's neat image would linger in shiny surfaces, her presence in the placement of the mother's collected objects. China. VHS cassettes. Individualized ketchup packets.

So when the mother left to her sister's, fretting and fussing about her home unwomanned for seven days, Amara summoned observations of the mother's immaculate obsession, and cleaned up. Fingernails for the crevasses of the fold-out tables and the faucet contours; don't forget the trunk of the toilet; scour the microwave's saffronsplotchy insides.

Amara awaited the mother's return, anxious for the praise that would legitimize her evening plans with a boy from school. Amara hoped to be alleviated by pre-empting cleanup time, so the mother could bask in a clean house and Amara could graciously step into her own life.

Every time the mother visited her sister, she came home alien. Beaming. Joyous. Like she had breathed deeply. Amara loved that foreign version of the mother. She wanted to be that fount, the source of smiles. But that day, she watched the remnants of sisterjoy drain from the mother's face as she surveyed her gleaming kitchen and uncluttered closets. Her brand new, Autumn Rain scented J-Cloth. Amara saw the familiar face of betrayal: disbelief, then mortification. Like she had stolen from the mother. The mother immediately donned pink plastic gloves, still sticky inside from the sweat of Amara's palms. She said nothing and did everything, again.

Amara sobbed, felt sorry for herself. She could not understand. She could not understand. If she could just name the mother's stagnating, stuttering fear, then at least it could be explicable, the vast pain of the woman constrained into a few little letters: Agoraphobia. PTSD. Depressed. She read these words, felt distant from the small and quiet, sad mother.

Eventually, Amara went out with that boy. He was blond and blue-eyed, carnivorous. Large, white and non-Muslim. She flirted, kissed, touched. He pushed her. She froze. No. He didn't care.

That boy raped Amara. Searing pain in tracers of blond and blue.

Suddenly, Amara cleaned constantly. She cleaned herself, every aspect of her life. She fought the mother in screeching battles about alphabetical order, about over-polishing, about draining the hot water tank four times a day. They both did that, stood naked and red in the blistering hot, camouflaging water.

Amara obsessed over soap. She bought bagfuls of it. The hypoallergenic kind: nothing in it, no chemicals, no possibility for dirt, nothing man-made. She desperately wanted a bar of soap that had no man in it, that had not been touched by a man, those thick fingers that had done her such disturbing harm; she just wanted to be clean without the remnants of his touch, and she didn't want to replace his touch with the touch leftover on that bar of soap. She called companies. Asked the drugstore clerk intently about the soap making procedure. "Yeah, I know what it's made of, but did anyone touch it? How did it get into the box? Who wrapped it?"

She sped soap home, eager to hide her stash of purity, a treasure in the filthy world. Amidst the cleaning war, a hiding spot was hard to come by. No corner piles offered cover. Amara paced to an unassuming drawer and wrenched it open without meaning to. Rage had asserted itself in Amara's actions.

The full and deep drawer harboured octagons or triangles or hearts, individually wrapped, a variety of pastel colours. Sample Soaps. The poor immigrant way to do what Amara had just done. When the mother needed to be clean she collected free sample soaps, a hidden drawerful.

And Amara wept, because she understood: They fought for the little control allotted to them, control over dirt and garbage and belongings. Control that was no control at all; control over the details of a predetermined action. Control over the intricacies of an expression of obedience. Not what their bodies did, just the manner in which their bodies did it.

Amara relinquished the battle for cleanup time and left to the dirty world. To years of drug-induced indifference. Someone's shed, someone's car, some street. Dirty places. Despite this paradigm shift from pristine to polluted, she obeyed the rules she formed early: be wary of men, take control and use fingernails. Amara remembered these lessons from the mother on her voyage into the grimy outside.

Old:

And when in this narrative do I get to say I? When does Amara become I; that border of memory and time, categorized by some achievement or failure, some change in me that was imperceptible then but now seems obvious (Of *course* I would divide my memories there, call that one "then" and this one "now," that one "young" and this one "old"). Moments pass, memories like merchandise rolling backwards on a conveyor belt, dropping unceremoniously into a pile of me-stuff. The Pile of Amara is not neat and tidy but haphazardly grows with memories once articulated in the first person. The character changes. In each moment that is now a memory, I edit out "I" and replace it with "Amara." For distance. Not her anymore, but always her.

I think of my mother when I am wracked with menstruation; the ache of womanhood binds me to her. The whole process of rearing humanity is painful. When we become women, the passage of life is marked monthly with paralyzing pain of the body and mind, so we never forget the rate of our deterioration. Then childbirth, then the struggle of raising another human and his torturous betrayals, because even the best of them move on. To the child for whom she sacrificed meaningful and productive years, she becomes an endearing afterthought, if she's lucky. Life beckons. And then the mother is alone, gladly or sadly.

My mother is at this stage. A solemn and solitary porcelain doll.

She drives me to unapologetic action. It is not what she says. It is who she is. I want to be the opposite in so many ways that I forget the ways in which I want to be her. Even her infinite patience and good nature, even her constant martyrdom and unselfish generosity do not appeal to me as traits I would adopt, because they are characteristics that enable her slavery. It is crippling, silencing. It is paralyzing out there. A world of poverty and ill will. Safer inside. She knows her demons and how to cope with them; how to lick her wounds so they don't get infected. She has adapted like an animal to its cage.

My mother is an animal in a zoo of humiliation and exploitation.

She is everything soft about me. From her I learned a woman's suffering, a woman's infinite unlimits. But I learned to fight on my own. I fight myself too, my condescension for her lot, my angry desire to shake her awake, to shove potential down her delicate throat.

I understand. Mother. I try to exert control in a man's world but it's fucking hard, it's a fight the whole way, but cleaning, that is easy. No one protests. No one argues. No one gets violent. I am allowed.

So I'm going to clean up the world. Just not the way they expect me to. They think I'm just cleaning up after them, mending the wounded they leave in my path. But I'm organizing the wounded to defend themselves next time and to defend another sufferer the time after. I'm learning how to make the fist of resistance even with broken fingers. I'm going to stop them from messing us up, stop them from splattering everywhere. I'm going to clean up. And every time I help another woman break free of her cage I remember yours, immaculate. A nice place to be imprisoned.

Far away from you, a dingy food court evokes the urgent grimace that would possess your lips and eyebrows at seeing (or smelling) the state of this place. Food courts, those necessary and jubilant, static places. They smell frayed and yellowed, like your J-Cloth. I come here to remind myself of the years of caked dirt caught in the creases, leftovers from the table's thousand patrons. This kind of dirt is easy to miss, unless you know to look there. But once you know to look, you can never forget the yawning crevasse, texture heavy with stickydust, that can be exorcised only by a fingernail.

It's cleanup time.

Christine Lowther

LIGHTEN UP

You move between love
and that essential solitude
you speak of, but I think you
know solitude only as you know
the sea in a handful of water.
— Pat Lowther, "Magellan"

After rolling me in your soft bed
you said *I want to be alone in my life*

In the drenching perfume of sweet-pea blossoms
you said *Maybe we should just stop.*

The comforting splash of the kingfisher
brings death to the minnow
and there is after all so much to thank you for:
the balm of betrayal
the shaming wash of rejection
the opportunity to grieve
astonishment at goodness in others

I want to be alone in my own life
something I could have mentioned
had I not been winding myself in unnecessary bandages

Why can't you just enjoy the moment? Lighten up?

By all means, if you have the time, allow me to explain.
It began on an island with arbutus trees
a middle-aged bespectacled man stood on a wharf, weeping,
his two young daughters crying and clinging to him.
Three uniformed strangers made some attempt to remove the girls;

a police boat was waiting.
He was begging the strangers to let him say goodbye to his children.
In the shallows beneath the wharf
       three river otters paused in their play.

Otters are like people.
Sometimes they travel in family clusters
other times they live alone.
I was the younger daughter
for my part I am a solitary animal
seeking clarity out the other side of pain

Oh, let it go, why don't you?
       Get over it.

What binds is the being left behind.
How to lighten up when desertion darkens down?
Oh to be lighthearted
and if a light heart takes wing
in perpetual flight from depth
so be it

"Lighten Up" was previously published in Christine's book, My Nature *(Leaf Press)*

Arleen Paré

ODE TO HAZEL WHITE

Her name, I learned, the Sunday morning she was buried
was Hazel White. Referred to in earlier reports simply
as a family friend just dropping by.
                              Shot in the back,
killed in a northern town by a husband not her own.
Bad luck, dropping by when the ex comes round with a shotgun.
How it was reported all that week: friend dropping by gets shot.
All week I puzzled at the happenstance:
was she sitting at the kitchen table having tea and
                he decided to shoot her
            instead?
Then Sunday morning radio (no one listening) reported her funeral.
Said how she died to protect her friend, stood with a plank
in her white-knuckled hands, against the man with a gun
outside the cabin where her friend lived with two daughters.
Hazel White warned him: you'll never get your wife
unless you get by me. That's what she said.
When he advanced
she swung
           and missed.
He shot her as she wheeled around, between the shoulder blades.
She gave her friend
                time to get away

Roy Roberts

THE WIFE KILLERS

We talk about it. Sit there,
Reg and I, shanked with disbelief
how easily some men kill their wives.
How can they do it?
We stare at the ground, there's nothing
that explains it for us.
We look into the sky. There's nothing.
Those guys are wired differently
than we are Roy.
I nod in agreement. What else?
We stare at the ground. Sit there
listen to an incomprehensible
howling in a hole we can't close.

Mildred Tremblay

THE NEIGHBOUR'S SON

Sly tormentor; two paths of constant snot
running down like larvae.
I tangled with him once
only. He snatched my licorice whip.
I kicked; he laughed,
caught my foot
held it
for as long as it took.

When I think of him now, I think
of the way I danced for him:

a one-legged doll.

Kate Braid

FRAMING JOB

On Friday, Art finishes up the pre-apprentice course by telling us how to find work.

"Go to Manpower. Tell them you want a job as carpenter's apprentice or a helper. When you go to the job site, wear your steel toes, carry your tool belt. Look ready to work."

I have seven dollars in the bank. So on Monday morning, I head to Manpower and tell the counsellor I want a job as apprentice carpenter. He asks how fast I can type. He is not joking. When I say again I want a job as apprentice, he says, "But you *can* type, can't you?"

So I go to a different office and this time I ask for a woman counsellor. She gives me a list of companies who are looking for either carpenter's helpers or apprentices.

At the first place I wear my steel-toed boots and carry my tool belt and when I knock on the foreman's door he's a little surprised but invites me in. I tell him I have two years' experience as a helper and just finished four months of a pre-apprentice course. He walks slowly around me, looking. I feel like a statue in a museum.

Finally, "What does your husband think of your doing this?" he says.

"I'm not married."

"What does your father think?"

At the second place, the foreman says he needs some office work done and asks if I can type.

The third place is more hopeful. It's a company called H&F who are framing condominiums in Burnaby and the foreman, Hal, says, "We don't need anyone today," but he doesn't ask if I can type.

I revisit Manpower.

"Go back," she says. "Every morning. Who they need changes every day."

So I go back the next morning and the next and soon it's routine: I turn up at the H&F site every day at 7:30 a.m. with my boots and tool belt and look for Hal.

Often I have to search for him on the site and once in a while I pass a man who's cleaner than most of the carpenters, wearing a white hard hat.

"White Hats," Art had told the class, "are either engineers or the site superintendent." After a while the White Hat and I recognize each other, nod.

One afternoon Rafael from the pre-apprentice class, phones.

"I just got a job!" He's elated. "With framers in Burnaby. Foreman's named Hal."

I freeze. "What's the name of the company?"

It's H&F, the same site, same Hal who'd said no to me again that morning.

Ten minutes later I'm on my way to the site wondering how I can make them hire me if they really don't want to. But fury carries me and I head onto the site, looking for Hal. I have no idea what I'll do when I find him but I'm halfway there when the White Hat, the superintendent, spots me.

"Come to start work?" he asks pleasantly.

"No."

He frowns. "I thought they hired someone today."

"They did. It was a friend of mine. A guy," I add, which doesn't matter to the superintendent I guess, but it does to me. I'm pissed off.

The super looks at me for one long minute. "I see," he says. "I have to walk that way anyway. You don't mind if I walk with you?"

I know an ally when I see one.

We spot Hal in front of a half-finished house, waving a set of plans. He looks surprised to see me. Before I can say anything, the superintendent smiles pleasantly and says, "I hear you're hiring, Hal."

Hal looks suspicious. "Hired a guy this afternoon," he says not to the super but to me. "Too bad you didn't come a little earlier."

"Any chance you could use someone else?" the superintendent asks. I can't believe my luck. The super is still smiling, his eyes now firmly fixed on Hal. Hal looks away, then at me, then points to a man balanced on the top plates of a two-storey building nearby, directing a crane as it lifts trusses.

"See that guy?" he says.

I nod.

"Think you could work up there?"

I have seven dollars in the bank. "Yes," I say.

"She can start then," he says not to me but to the superintendent. "Tomorrow at seven. Ten dollars an hour. Unless you don't want to work six days a week?"

"That's fine," I say, but I can hardly talk. Euphoria is threatening to cut off my windpipe.

"Tomorrow then," and Hal turns on his heel. He doesn't look happy.

"A few things I want to talk to you about, Hal," the superintendent says, and follows him.

"Thank you," I say to his back. A thousand thank-yous! as I walk around the lumber piles to my truck, my heart pounding. I have a job putting roofs on, the one job I hated most at school, balancing on two-by-fours with a sheer drop on either side. But it's a job.

~

The next morning it isn't exactly terror I feel as I lace up my boots and drive to work at 6:30 a.m. but terror is here, buried under the small voice that asks why they didn't hire me sooner, wonders how I'm going to walk those top plates. Like a razor's nick, it bleeds all the way to the job.

The site is a development of perhaps a hundred units, all with concrete basements and two wood-framed storeys. I park on the dirt road in front of the foreman's shack. The two houses in front of me bristle with labourers carrying two-by-fours onto a new platform, ready for framing. But something is wrong. Hal said they start at 7:00 a.m. but my watch says 6:45.

"You're late," he snaps behind me. "The boss likes you here early." He points down the road to the house he showed me the day before. This morning the man on top of the walls shares the heights with a bundle of trusses. I recognize their bony angles jutting over the edge.

"Dave," Hal says, and is gone.

Dave wears blue jeans, a white T-shirt and no hard hat and he's walking backward on the top plates, laying out where the trusses will go. In school, Art always said a good carpenter is ready for anything. He said some carpenters never get to build a roof in their whole lives. Right now Art would say I'm lucky.

When I reach the house where Dave is working I'm shaking slightly with the chill of the morning. I wait for him to notice me. When he doesn't, I call up, "Dave?" My voice sounds small.

No answer. I clamber through the opening that will one day be the front door.

All around me the sounds of his working ricochet and boom inside bare walls. It reminds me of the houses I played in as a child, only this time I'm not sneaking in after supper hoping the watchman won't spot me; this time I have a right to be here. I climb a wooden ladder to the second floor which is covered with leftover ends of lumber, nails and torn cardboard from nail boxes. Art was fastidious about cleanliness. It keeps a job safe, he said. My head is barely through the opening in the floor when Dave barks, "I need spikes!"

I find an empty coffee tin in the rubbish on the floor and fill it from the fifty-pound box of three-and-a-half-inch nails in one corner, trip as I cross the floor to where a decrepit ladder lies against one wall. I half-carry, half-drag the ladder to the wall where Dave is working, but by the time I have it in place he's on the opposite side. Should I stay where I am or move the ladder to where he is? I put the ladder up where I am and climb and Dave is back, throwing the contents of the tin into his belt with one quick motion. (Have I brought enough?) I feel ridiculously proud of myself. Dave flips the tin to the floor where it bounces and rolls to a corner.

"Up here," he barks.

"Here" is the two-by-four that forms the top of the framed wall.

I know a little about trusses, the great pre-built triangles of two-by-four wood that act as rafters for the roof above and ceiling for the room below. We erected some at school. Now Dave has marked the plate at sixteen-inch centres.

"Hurry up!"

Now. Now I have to climb to the top of this ladder and stand and walk along a three-and-a-half-inch-wide board. And sometimes I'll have to walk it back-wards, as Dave is doing now, finishing marking centres. I'll walk it in my over-sized men's boots and I'll ignore the two-storey drop to the ground on one side and the littered plywood floor one storey below, on the other.

I can't do this!

But I'm damned if I'm going to make them hire me, and then just turn around and say I can't do it. And there's the matter of the seven dollars. So I climb to the top of the ladder, place my boots on the wall, let go my hands and slowly straighten.

The air is thin up here and of a strange temperature that swings wildly be-tween hot and cold. I smell fresh-cut lumber, sharp as smelling salts and I can see for miles, looking south past the development, across the flats and right on out to where early morning mist still hides the airport. A breeze washes my cheeks. I am a tightrope walker with no net.

"Grab a truss!"

And now I'm being asked to fly.

Standing still wasn't so bad but moving is a different matter. Arms spread, each foot excruciatingly placed, I walk like the newest member in the high-wire act, slowly, to the end of the wall, ease myself into a crouch and lay my hands on the pile of trusses. Dave waits, casually perched on the opposite wall. I know the past minute screams novice but I don't care. If I'm going to die here, at least I've lasted this long.

"The top one goes to the far end of the building."

I look behind me, horrified. The end of the building is sixty feet away.

But he's already pulling at the truss, bouncing it violently to free it. The whole building rocks and the sound booms and echoes in the drum of the framed box beneath us. Afraid he's going to throw me off, I slide back and with one hand holding the wall, with the other I poke at the truss to help free it on my side. The fact that it finally comes loose has nothing to do with me. Then Dave half-lifts, half-pushes it along the length of the wall while I mostly follow, reaching out when I can spare a hand from balancing, to give a token push. When it sticks, halfway along, he gives it another bounce that shakes the building so I cling again, terrified he'll tumble me off. When he finally gets it to the end he yells, "Three spikes in each!"

My feet are huge and always in the way of the hammer. The first nail bends and takes forever to pull out again, braced as I am on nothing, worried about applying too much leverage and toppling myself over. I've just started the second spike when I look up and Dave has already driven his three nails, braced the truss with a piece of one-by-four and is now turning back for the next.

And that's how it goes all morning as I mostly do nothing except stay alive and follow the trusses as Dave forces them one at a time along the wall. I manage to nail.

Jancis M. Andrews

JANCIS'S EXTRA-RICH DESSERT

A carpenter ant has climbed my kitchen counter
eager to whoop it up with my grasshopper pie.
Such a glittering ebony body! Such a big, black
helmeted head! Darth Vader
on six hydro-pole legs!
I truly regret having to kill him
in order to discourage his relatives.
But in death I give him
what I denied in life,
and for his final resting place, tuck him
into the dark-chocolate crumb crust
which soon I will serve
to the female guest who asked down her nose,
My dear, whatever do you housewives do
to amuse yourselves
all day long?

"*Jancis's Extra-Rich Dessert*" *appeared in* Canadian Woman Studies, *Vol.13, No.*
3 , 1993

Dawn Service

THE VILLAGE IDIOT

In a small clearing of juvenile pine on the north shore of Nimpo Lake, at the end of a long, muddy, rutted driveway sat a small log cabin with a rolled tar-paper roof. A screen door opened to the porch where a mammoth-sized propane refrigerator stood guard over stacks of empty beer cases and fishing poles. The porch screen sagged, torn from the corners. Inside, the honey-coloured logs had been chinked with insulation and covered with strips of quarter-round. A tin bucket sat atop the woodstove next to a propane cook stove. There was a short run of cupboards with a sink that drained into a slop bucket. Nestled beside a window that looked out over the lake was an unfinished pine table, ring-stained from coffee cups.

It was my boyfriend Bree's cabin and we'd recently just met. Both of us were refugees from failed marriages and bygone places. It was my first summer in the Chilcotin and I'd hired him to install the windows and door on my own cabin on nearby Anahim Lake. He was a carpenter. I'd always wanted to marry one. The intimate play between a mind that could figure trigonometry and hands that could take a pliable board and shape it into something useful, even artful, and in the process create the most delicious smell was worthy of my reverence. He lent me his tools, showed me how to design a set of stairs using rise over run and how to frame a stud wall. He hauled log slabs in his truck from the debris pile, helped me cut and nail them together to use as a frame for the privy pit. We worked side by side and his cabin became the semblance of a home I didn't have. Dinner at a table. Dishes in a sink. His bed was where I read at night beneath the hiss of a propane light.

Bree introduced the old man to me. He drove down the driveway, approached the cabin on his scooter, a man in his seventies, partially bald with a puffy round face, sag in the jowls, shifty downcast eyes. His cabin was just down the road and when Bree first took me there, he left me alone with his wife while he and the old man went out back to the workshop. They were retired folks Bree had known from the Lower Mainland. I stood in the doorway of their cabin and admired the wood cook stove in their kitchen.

"You're a teacher," his wife said to me. "Well then, you should be smart enough to see for yourself. He had a nice wife." Her contemptuous tone suggested hostility so I left the cabin and went to the workshop.

It was a shrine to the tool gods and to the gods of perfect order. Everything had its place and was in it. There were little drawers that slid open to reveal nuts, bolts, screws and nails, and not one screw in a nail drawer or bolt in a nut drawer. It reminded me of the home of a friend I once had, whose obsession with perfection was best illustrated by the box that sat next to the woodstove. Inside were small rectangular pieces of white paper that had been cut with scissors, twisted in the centre so that they resembled little bow ties. They were used to start the fire. Each tiny twist held the sad spirit of her need to tidy up the world because she herself was in complete turmoil.

The two of them stood just inside the door, each with a beer in hand. The old man was exalting his own virtue through the power of his possessions and the order in which he'd arranged them. Later Bree told me it's where the old man drank in secret.

I heard the sound of his scooter in the driveway several times that first summer I spent in the Chilcotin. He'd drive in, bark out his pompous pretensions, then drive away. He drove up and down the entire neighbourhood, in and out of people's driveways, had assigned himself the job of local caretaker, self-appointed protector of all unoccupied cabins.

Alone at the edge of the dance floor at the community barbeque, with Bree gone to get another beer, I stood watching the band until he slipped in front of me.

"I've been dreaming about you," he said.

I walked away, found Bree and told him what the old man had said.

"Just ignore him," Bree said. "He's an idiot."

I ignored him, continued to ignore him, including the day he drove down the driveway on his scooter, stopped and opened the left side of his vest to expose a handgun in a holster.

In bed with the flu the day Bree went to work at Charlotte Lake without me, I heard the sound of a small engine come down the driveway and knew it wasn't Bree's diesel truck rattling back for something he'd forgotten. The sound of footsteps ascending the porch steps and the creak of the porch-door hinges sent me bolting out of bed to lock the door but just as I got there, the person on the other side pressed down on the latch and pushed it open. There he stood with his left hand on the door handle and his right on the end of the barrel of a shotgun he'd just leaned against the wall beside the door. Without an invitation, he pushed open the door and sat down at the kitchen table with a flushed face looking both confused and angry, eyes darting back and forth across the floor, as if they weren't sure what was going to happen next.

It seemed as though the rules of a civil society didn't have any place in the Chilcotin. It seemed as though summer residents from other places thought that the Chilcotin was the *Last Frontier*, and that made it entirely acceptable to pack around handguns or shotguns or invade people's property, or enter their house without knocking or being invited, because when you're on vacation, there are no rules. People shot bears out of trees, birds out of the sky and a guy on Nimpo Lake once blasted a flock of mergansers out of the water because they ate trout. And when his neighbour complained to the other neighbours that someone was shooting ducks, the shooter marched over and told him they weren't ducks, but "fucking mergansers," and asked couldn't he "tell the fucking difference?"

"What do you want?" I asked the intruder. "I've got the flu and don't want any company."

He mumbled something, shook his head, left red-faced. I bolted the door and went back to bed.

When I recovered from the flu a few days later, I got up early one morning to make our lunch for a workday at Charlotte Lake. It was 6:00 a.m. when I looked out the kitchen window and saw him sitting on his scooter at the end of the driveway looking at the cabin.

"What the hell is he doing there?" Bree asked.

He turned and drove away. On our way to Charlotte Lake, we stopped to find out what he wanted. His wife answered the door.

"What were you doing in my driveway this morning?" Bree asked.

He crept behind his wife, held his pointer finger to his lips and pursed them as if to say *Sssshhhh!*

We left their cabin and drove to Charlotte Lake.

On Saturday, in the Nimpo Lake bakery where I went to buy bread, he and his wife stood in line ahead of me. He saw me come through the door, started a booming diatribe in front of the other customers at the bakery.

"I saw your boyfriend driving 120 miles an hour between Anahim and Nimpo the other day," he barked. "Can't he get his ass out of bed in the morning to get to work on time?"

I went to the second-hand store to get away from them, but they drove right in behind me. I watched his wife in the store, wondered how it was possible to remain married to such a man.

The next time I saw him he was parked in my driveway. I'd been in town getting groceries and when I drove down my driveway, he was sitting in his truck in my yard.

"I just came to see what you're doing on your cabin," he said.

Despite the flagrant show of firearms, I didn't think he was dangerous. I kept denying what was right in front of my face. I showed him the sanding I was doing and the loft floor I'd installed. He looked around, said it was a nice place, stepped forward, put his arm around me and planted his lips on my face.

"I've been dreaming about you," he said. "When I wake up in the morning I think it's you in bed beside me."

I told him he'd better not tell Bree what he'd just said, referring to the flag of betrayal he'd be waving, and he said, "*You'd better not tell either*," and I realized he considered my remark a conspiratorial invitation.

"You need to leave," I said.

It was time to wrap up the plot. I called his wife, asked her to tell him to come to Bree's cabin so we could have a chat with him. "Six p.m.," I said.

Alone outside in the yard at 5:00 p.m.—Bree not home yet—I saw the old man's truck coming down the driveway. He got out, marched towards the door.

"You were told to come at six," I said, "You need to come back at six."

"This is between you and me," he said, and continued to march toward the door.

"There's nothing between you and me," I said. "Get out of here and don't come back till six." He left.

A few minutes before 6:00 p.m., I heard the rattling relief of a truck's diesel engine in the driveway.

"He was here," I said. "I told him to come back at six."

When he returned he was invited to sit down at the kitchen table, accepted the coffee I offered. Bree asked him why he was shouting diatribes in the bakery and that it probably wasn't a good thing to do because he was a professional carpenter and didn't need disparaging diatribes shouted about the community. He backpedalled calmly through a flat sea of denial, until we moved on to the provocative language, his misplaced hands. Lips.

Red isn't really an apt description of the colour his face changed. It began as red but changed to purple as the veins on his neck bulged.

"You fucking liar. You psycho fucking bitch," he shouted then denied, swore, shouted again.

I went outside, listened through an open window, waited for a resolution that wasn't forthcoming so I went back inside. "I've had enough of you," I said. "Get out of here."

He stood up, reached into his pocket, pulled out a disk-shaped device in his palm. "Ha, ha, I've got it all on tape," he said. "This is a secret recorder."

As he stepped toward the door, he shouted, "You keep her away from my house or I'll fucking shoot her." He climbed into his truck and rolled down the window. "She comes anywhere near my house, I'll fucking shoot her."

I wondered why he addressed me in the third person rather than directly. It was curious how he thought I might want to go anywhere near his house.

"Get in the truck," Bree said. "We're going to the RCMP."

It took several months to get a search warrant for the handgun, arrest him and place a restraining order on him. By the time they did, he and his wife had gone back to their winter residence in the Lower Mainland.

"Is that your man?" Corporal Fisk asked me as he placed the file in front of me at the RCMP detachment in Anahim Lake.

"That's him," I said, but the mug shot showed a much humbler-looking man. The face was a familiar red but the eyes were subdued and vulnerable. The cock was all gone from his doodle-doo.

"Did they find the handgun?" I asked.

"They found a lot of weapons but not the handgun," he said.

"It's hidden somewhere on his Nimpo Lake property. Why didn't they search that?" He didn't know.

"So what happens now?" I asked.

"He's been charged and Crown counsel will begin gathering evidence for the trial. If they don't think the case will lead to a conviction they may stay the charges," he said.

"Why would they charge him, incarcerate him, confiscate his guns and then not proceed with a trial?" I asked.

"They weigh the evidence and decide on the likelihood of a conviction. It takes up their time and costs a lot of money to proceed with a trial. They must be fairly confident of a conviction," he said. "Were you drinking when it happened?"

"I was drinking tea," I said. "Bree was drinking beer."

"Not a credible witness," he said. "It's your word against his."

"What about the restraining order?" I asked.

"There's a restraining order, which prevents him from entering either of your properties."

The following spring, the couple returned to their cabin with an *alleged transcript* of the tape he said he'd secretly recorded that night in the cabin. He took it to every home on Nimpo Lake, tried to reverse his role from predator to victim. A woman whom I thought was a friend told me to stay away from a community function because he'd be there. I went anyway and when I arrived she pretended not to know me. A man at the Dean River canoe race, a friend of the predator, walked toward me with clenched fists and taut jaw muscles, stood in my personal space and glared. My voyeuristic neighbour told people in the community to stay away from me. *She's bad news*, she said.

Later in the privacy of my cabin, the predator's neighbour, a senior bachelor, told me the same man had once come to his house, passed him a bullet and said, "Go ahead, why don't you do everybody a favour."

Years later the predator spent a night in the Anahim Lake jail for domestic violence. He'd been drinking and beat his wife.

I saw him again years later with his wife at the local store. I stood at my post office box, flipped through my mail. He paced up and down the aisles, like a caged animal, avoided eye contact. She stood still, looked directly at me. Smirked.

Auto Jansz

COMMUNITY DANCE IN NORTHERN ONTARIO

As told to Emma Cochrane

Editor's Note: Names of people and places, and dates have been omitted.

It was in northwestern Ontario, and it was in the nineties, I think. I was working at the Indian Friendship Centre, and I chose to go up there from Victoria to work on my chapbook. I needed to be somewhere secluded, quiet and peaceful, so that's where I went. And I knew people up there already. I had friends and they were like family.

It's just a small, white and native community. Half and half. It's a mining town. The mines weren't active at the time I was living there, so it's just a bunch of houses thrown on land. And it's funny 'cause they just kind of had to carve streets out of whatever they thought looked like a street. But, yeah, just a lot of mobiles and houses. And the main street, there are lights up there now, I believe. I guess the main street is the highway coming in, and then it just sort of forks, and one road goes and goes and then ends, and the other one goes and goes and ends. So, there's no other way out of that town except through that one road.

There was one bar, which I liked to frequent, and it was run by some neat old girls. And, it was kinda weird coming in there 'cause there was this big partition. And, I thought, what's up with this big partition? So, everyone's welcome but only the white men could be on one side and the natives and white women were allowed on the other side.

But the dances are a hoot. You'd just go and dance your face off. And sometimes they'd have polka dances, but mostly it was mainstream music and you'd have a few drinks and you'd laugh with your friends. A lot of group dances 'cause line dancing was big at that point. It was just all canned music, and it was a place to go and rip it up a little bit. They were always fun, except for that one night, it was kind of a weird night.

So, I just want to say that I was pretty openly gay up there—I didn't have a lot to hide. I didn't have a girlfriend and I didn't really give a shit about what people thought because I knew a lot of the people from when I lived there before—I used to work for the Ministry of Natural Resources many, many years before. And those same folk were still up there. And my buddy, he's gay and there were a few other gay guys up there. Actually, there were quite a few gay men up there. And there were, like, four lesbians up there. The lesbians never came out to the dances, but the guys did. And there wasn't a lot of tension about that because we were all pretty social and just sort of, you know, living, living our lives. And, if you got a problem, deal with it. Don't deal with me, deal with your problem, you know? And being at the Friendship Centre, it was a pretty open place and people would rent the hall. You just get more on a heart-to-heart and mind-to-mind level, and those were the sorts of relationships I had up there. And just casual talks with acquaintances but my circle was comfortable and safe and so it was a good life up there. I really enjoyed it.

One night, I was out with my buddies—and I was having a really good time—and then this guy, I don't know, what the fuck. I can't remember his name now, but he just kind of tapped me on the ass. And I just turned around and said, "What the fuck is your problem?" And he was just like, heh huh hee ha, and just stayed laughing with a couple of his buddies. So I thought, okay, whatever.

And then, it happened again. And I just sort of turned around and said, "Fuck you. Now fuck off."

So, I moved and, at that point, when I moved, they followed and did it again. And, in my head, I thought, you fucking bastards. You're stalking me. So, I got louder and I threw my drink at them, and I said, "Get the fuck out of here you fucking perverts." More people noticed and I guess they split. It was such a long time ago, I can't remember the details.

I went up and told the boys, "What the fuck? My ass was just grabbed. Three times, maybe four, I don't know. Everything happened so fast. But, they weren't that close. They'd just [grabbing gesture] and run back." The boys asked, "Who did it?" I said, "I don't know, some fucking moron. I don't know where he is. He's gone now. He's white with a belly. That's all I remember, you know?" I said, "I'm outta here, I'm going home."

And I remember walking home, and I thought, fuck, now I'm walking home—and I lived on the same street [as the dance]—they're gonna see where I live if they happen to go by. So then I got paranoid.

Anyway, I got home, and I just kinda calmed down. And I'd forgotten about it and then my buddy and I went for a hike the next day and I—something was just, like, biting at me. And I said, "You know, I think I am fucking pissed off." And he said, "Well, what are you gonna do about it?" And I said, "I don't know."

That was Sunday; the dance was on Saturday. I get to work Monday and I'm still pissed off. And I still got this thing biting at me. And it was mostly women working there and every day we'd all sit around and well, they'd talk mostly, I'd just listen. But everyone just kind of had coffee and took a good hour and a half to get the workday going. And they said, "Well, how was your weekend?" And I said, "Well, this happened to me." And then B said, "What did he look like?" And I said, "Well, I don't know. He was white with a belly. And he was in his twenties, I guess." And she said, "The same thing happened to my sister, only it was worse. He cornered her when she was coming up from the bathroom from downstairs, him and his buddies." And I said, "You're kidding. I wanna talk to her."

So, we got together and we spoke Monday. She said, "Yeah I have another friend, too, and the same thing happened—just cornering and sexual blah blahs." And I said, "Well, fuck this. Let's fucking do something about this."

So, we did. We went to the police station. And I think we went separately and then, the next thing I know, he's in jail and he's going away for six months. Then his name's in the newspaper. He had just months prior witnessed his girlfriend being run down and cut open by a snowmobile. His girlfriend of high school. His buddy was drunk behind the bars and was just like revving it and *smack*—pinned her up against a truck and cut her open. So, I mean he was dealing with his shit, right. But still, doesn't give him the right to be a fucking idiot.

And it just sort of released itself after that. As soon as the three of us spoke, I just thought, okay we have to do something, and they wanted to. But, I think they were a little scared because they knew his history and it was like, oh, it's just blah blah, don't worry about it. But they were affected as well, and I said, "Well, I'm going to do this. Let's just do it. It'll be more of an impact if the three of us say something." And, I don't really know, something more must have happened to the other girls for him to go to jail 'cause he tapped my ass, but he cornered B's sister and I don't know what he did to the other woman. And, at that point, I knew people that were going in and out of jail all the time. And this one guy was like, "I'm gonna fuck him up 'cause I'm going into jail in a few days too." And I said, "Yeah, go for it. Fuck him up." But yeah, after that, I felt like there was closure. There was closure because it became public. It wasn't embarrassing, and maybe he got something out of it when he was in jail. Maybe there was some kind of counselling considering what he'd just experienced.

After Auto shared this story, she realized she might still have the original police report somewhere in a box of journals and writing. She found it immediately. The following is an excerpt from her statement recorded only a few days after the incident, outlining a much more violent and threatening scenario than she remembered:

At around 11:00 p.m., I arrived at the hall with my friend, J. We walked into the dance hall and J went and sat at the first table on the left as you walk into the hall. I was standing at the end of the table.

At around 11:20 p.m., J's friends got up and left and J went off and visited, leaving me alone standing at the table. I was facing the stage where the music was when I felt someone reach between my legs and grab my crotch, squeezing me between the legs. I turned around and said, "What the hell do you think you're doing?"

This guy was wearing a darker colour baseball cap. Having fairly short brownish sandy, light-colour hair, which was cut around the eyes. He wasn't wearing glasses and he didn't have a moustache, he had a baby face, it being chubby. His whole body was heavy-set and he was about six feet tall. He was wearing a white T-shirt and a jean jacket and jeans. He replied "What are you, a dyke? What are you, a dyke?"

I was very pissed off at his touching me in that spot and for his saying that to me. I didn't say anything back, as I didn't want to cause a scene. I then walked away to the other side of the hall to the third or fourth table in front of the bar. I was standing in front of the table facing the stage when I felt someone again reach from behind between my legs and squeeze my crotch. I turned around and it was the same guy that had grabbed my crotch before. He was laughing and smiling. I walked away. I was feeling confused. I didn't want to leave because of him. I moved again back to where I had been the first time because I was intimidated by him and wanted to get away. I was standing there keeping my eye on this fellow and then after about ten minutes I was not paying any attention to him any more and suddenly like he had snuck up on me from behind like the previous two times, and I was again grabbed between my legs having my crotch squeezed.

I turned and it was the same guy that had grabbed me the two previous times. There were again no words exchanged. He was smiling or laughing. I was worried at this point because I felt I was being preyed upon and that he was following me. After that I walked over to the door by the bar where J and R were standing. I told J what happened and then I left. I was kind of scared when I left. I wanted to get out before the dance was over and this guy saw where I lived. I ran all the way home. ...

Fiona Tinwei Lam

HEADLINES

A newsprint story on your pillow,
just a reminder
to be careful.

> Girl found unconscious underneath a bush,
> head mashed in with a bottle
> after the party, who can't remember
> what he did to her.

> Single mother in basement suite
> who wouldn't scream
> in case it woke her babies.
> He found them anyway.

> Fourteen-year-old girl, locked for four months
> in her neighbour's cellar, emerging
> in the photograph, hair matted like old grass,
> eyes like filmed-over gashes.
> He'd throw down sandwiches
> just before leading the daily search for her.

Some nights, before you go to sleep,
your mother sits beside you and grips your arm.
She asks about what she's given you,
then says

when the Japanese invaded,
the women in the Hong Kong house
smeared themselves
with feces and urine
before the soldiers came to the door
on their hunt for women.

From the way she looks at you,
she already sees the worlds ahead
unfurling their possibilities
of men and moments when
the women's faces will be yours.

FILM LOOP

At the wheel of a green Toyota
a woman is careening into rage
frame by frame.

Three stony children sealed inside.
She wants to smash
them into gratitude,
smack them
against widowhood.

A sudden blur of speed—
heads arc forward,
jerk back,
the ebb and flow of possible
oblivions.

The daughter turns to glare
from the screen on the wall
at the invisible witness
who will not save her
from this re-living
this re-dying.

"Headlines" and "Film Loop" were previously published in Fiona's book Intimate
Distances *(Nightwood Editions)*

Elizabeth Haynes

THE ALCHEMIST

WARNING: *Women tourists should not in any circumstances take tours on their own or in pairs with independent guides but should stick to larger group tours run by reputable agencies.*
—Lonelyplanet.com on Bolivian jungle tours.

We drift toward the camp spot just as dusk is settling on the brown Ibare River. Fish splash the still water. Papacho noses the boat into the bank then jumps out to haul it in. I scan for the crocodiles I've seen all afternoon slipping down the mud and into the drink. Papacho motions me out and we hike up to a clearing on the edge of the jungle where we will spend the night.

It's dark when Papacho begins setting up a tiny pup tent. Where is mine? I ask, having insisted on two tents when I hired him in the jungle town of Trinidad in Bolivia to take me up this tributary of the Mamoré River. One tent is better, he says. One tent is not better, I say. You will be frightened, he says. I will not be frightened, I say. There are caiman, jaguar, bear, he says. My country is full of bears, I say. We haven't passed a single boat all day. We are miles from anywhere.

I know nothing about this man except that his sister ran the hostel where I stayed. That exactly one waiter and one travel agent said he was a good guide. I wandered the dusty streets of Trinidad looking for other backpackers who might want to ply a river. For days, I sat in the ice cream parlour at the edge of the plaza, watching cars and motorcycles roar by and listening to sound systems trying to out "*La Vida Loca*" each other. Listening to church bells, which rang for ten minutes, took a break for five and resumed on the quarter hour. I searched for tourists among tidy families who strolled the plaza, knots of teenagers at the *heladería*, but found no one.

Well, there was one other woman. A Frenchwoman I'd see striding around town or out to the Laguna Suárez in a pair of long hiking shorts, a button-down shirt, wool knee socks and a safari hat. She was heading to Guayamerín but told me she'd met a New Zealand couple who wanted to do a river trip. They, however, eluded me.

I debated with myself: *You've come all this way to go on a river, just hire him. It's stupid to go on your own. Papacho seems like a nice guy—but what about the German girl who was raped by her guide in Rurrenabaque? Papacho doesn't speak English—but it could be a great opportunity to practise your Spanish. You've been travelling for six months and nothing bad has happened to you—but what about the bus hijacking in Mexico? That was years ago and it was because you took a night bus.*

Shut up, I told the voices and over yet another dish of chocolate ice cream, I wrote down the pros and cons. The pros won, so I hired Papacho to take me down the river.

The first day of our trip came—as did Papacho, two hours late, on a borrowed motorcycle with no gear.

"*Desafortunadamente*," his friend had borrowed the motor from his boat to go fishing. He would take me to the town of Loreto to see the old Jesuit mission instead, and we would be on the river early the next day. We bumped down dusty roads, stopping to look at Jabiru storks, egrets and herons on the Pampas. An anteater ran across our path, forcing him to slam on the brakes and me to crash into his back.

Maybe it was me hanging on to his waist for dear life as other motorcycles and trucks roared by pelting us with stones and dust that gave him the "one tent" idea. Or maybe it was because I bought him a beer in Loreto while we ate *gallina picante*, hen with hot sauce, as their sisters pecked the scrubby yard. Or maybe it was just because I was a gringa alone.

The next day, the motor restored, we set off. Just me, Papacho and Gabriel García Márquez—in the form of a tattered copy of *One Hundred Years of Solitude* I'd found in Santa Cruz de la Sierra. I swung in the hammock he'd rigged for me, alternately watching the river and reading, smugly thinking it was fitting to read a book set in a remote jungle town while travelling through remote jungle. Would Papacho and I, like the novel's hero, José Arcadio Buendía, discover a Spanish galleon rooted in stone, a lushness of flowers and trees growing inside it? José Arcadio thought he had found a town surrounded by water on all sides. I was surrounded by water on all sides. Every so often Papacho called, "*Mira*," and I'd look up to see the rose-coloured fin of a *bufeo*, a pink dolphin, disappearing into brown, or a stork, its long legs hanging brokenly, cutting across the sky over the river.

We stopped for a midday lunch of piranha and hiked to a lagoon. The air was close. Papacho cut through the undergrowth with his machete until we got to the edge of the lagoon. "If a caiman attacks you," he said, "wait until it is close and then dive underneath it." Absolutely.

We stopped for an afternoon swim. "*Hay cocodrilos aquí?*" I asked. "No," Papacho said, adding that they only attack people when they're very hungry. I noticed he was in and out of the tea-coloured water in record time. I followed suit, retreating to my hammock to read my book, where Colonel Aureliano had decided to retreat from the world to become an alchemist, to fashion tiny fish out of gold.

Maybe the tent problem with just miscommunication. Papacho didn't speak English. I found his Spanish hard to understand and perhaps he found mine the same. Maybe I wasn't using the right words. The word for tent, *tienda*, also means store. The other word for tent, *carpa*, also means carp. I'd asked, "*Hay dos tiendas? Hay dos carpas?*" Are there two tents? Are there two stores? Are there two fish? Or perhaps I'd said, "*Muy necesito mi propia carpa.*" I really need my own carp. He'd answered, "*Sí, claro,*" meaning, perhaps, that he'd bring his fishing rod, he'd catch me one.

Or perhaps he had expectations. Did the gringas he brought down this river come to his *tienda* in the middle of the night, like the women who'd silently slip into the tent of the war hero, Colonel Aureliano, to partake of his genetic bounty?

Papacho disappeared over the bank. Huddling in the dark and slapping at mosquitoes, the voices in my head resumed: *You can sleep in the boat—so can the crocodiles. You can take the boat—good luck starting the motor; it takes Papacho ten minutes. He's been nice so far—yeah, so was the man in the bus station who sold you the ticket on that Mexican bus that was hijacked.*

I shiver in the dark, slap mosquitoes, put on a sweater. What the heck is Papacho doing down there, getting into something more comfortable? Just as I decide I'll sleep in the boat, crocodiles or no crocodiles, he appears with a flash-light and a rolled-up tarp. You sure you want your own tent? he asks. "*Absoluto,*" I say. I think I'm saying "absolutely" but I could also be saying "pure alcohol." He smiles as if to say, you can't blame a guy for trying, unrolls the tarp and pulls out a second tent. As we shake it out, my shoulders and stomach muscles unclench, Just as they did when the hijackers finished robbing us and left us lying on the cold ground in the middle of a field. Just as the stomachs of the women in Marquez's story did when their husbands returned from the wars.

Outside this ring of light, a dolphin jumps, crocodiles slide in and out of the water, something snorts. A bear? A caiman? The patron saint of careless gringas? The ghost of Colonel Aureliano? Papacho himself, perhaps.

Harvey Jenkins

ISOLATION

Patchy ownership of farmland,
some acres near our door, others
too far to see beside distant railway tracks or
running lengths along old gravel roads.
An accumulation of past disputes,
unspoken feuds, a grandparent's
badly worded will plus
something about a correction line.
One neighbour tosses dust clouds
near our backyard,
draws tighter and tighter circles
but never waves; never invited in for coffee.
Uncle Bob's red barn within sight
but he only visits once a year
to pay his portion
of the family's cemetery plot.
When father takes the truck into town,
the car's engine is disabled
so mother will always be home
to greet him.

"Isolation" first appeared in One Sweet Ride: An Easy Writers' Anthology *(Ascent Aspirations Publishing)*

Madeline Sonik

THE BONE GAME

Tanushri gives birth to a daughter, even though she should have given birth to a son. She had obeyed her late mother's instructions and ate red, salty meat each day of her pregnancy, even though she hated the sinewy texture of animal flesh, even though the thought of any creature being killed for its carcass brought despair to her heart; her mother had written with such authority from her death-bed. "You must eat the meat as raw as you possibly can, remove any bones and place them in a cloth sack, then tie the sack and tuck it under the foot of your bed." It had worked for Tanushri's sisters as well as for all her aunts, but this time, obviously, it had failed.

When Tanushri's husband, Anil, arrives at the hospital, Tanushri has almost recovered from her tears, but when he expresses his grave disappointment, both in their child and in their marriage, her sobbing begins again. Not only had Tanushri failed to bear a son, but since their wedding twelve months before, he points out, she has totally let her appearance go. She has become fat. Her face puffy, her eyes shrivelled and red from all the tears she's shed.

"Would it hurt," Anil asks, "to comb your hair, to put on a bit of lipstick, to make yourself look presentable for your husband?"

Privately Anil laments the fact he selected a bride solely on the strength of photographs his father had assembled. He values beauty greatly in women and Tanushri was, by far, the loveliest flower in the bouquet. But the flower went to seed and there was nothing other than beauty she possessed. She is not an educated woman and cannot speak intelligently about current events or literature. When he attempts to discuss his problems, Tanushri makes the most naive remarks, demonstrating constantly her ignorance of worldly matters and her childish views on human nature. She spends her time pining for her family and grieving for her dead mother, and seems incapable of adjusting to North American life. She cannot keep house, nor grocery shop alone, and she sets fire to virtually every meal she cooks.

When Tanushri arrives home with the fretful baby, Anil's sorrows only multiply. The child, whom Tanushri calls Tejas, is singularly without charm. Anil has never seen an infant like it. Most babies have some beguiling quality or other—some inherent appeal that nature furnishes as fortification against parental unkindness and neglect—but this child possesses none. It does not have the wide innocent eyes of an infant, its cheeks are not chubby and round, its nose is not a tiny jewel and its lips are nothing like a rosebud. In fact, its features are startlingly sharp like a hawk's. But this alone is not to blame for the child's appearance—it is also the set of her eyes, the slant of her jaw, the distance between her nose and lip—all of these things conspire in bringing about an appearance that is more than simply unattractive. This baby, which Anil has fathered and which Tanushri has borne, is decidedly mean-looking, and it pains Anil's heart to gaze at her, yet it fills him with guilt when he looks away.

"What kind of father am I?" he sobs, after drinking a glass of sweet grape wine. "What kind of husband?" he torments himself, falling further into wretchedness. It is as if his shame and misery are flames, and the wine is the only substance that might put them out. So he sits in his small study and drinks and weeps, compulsively recounting his misfortunes and obsessively berating himself.

Anil's dejection spills beyond his study, into the kitchen, where he finds Tanushri and beats her for his woes. At first, it is nothing more than a series of shoves but it rapidly becomes a smack, then a punch, then a kick, for which, he feels even more desolate and embarrassed about afterward. But it is only when Anil breaks Tanushri's nose and she must be admitted to the hospital that Anil realizes his personal disgrace can no longer remain private. The police arrest him and lock him in a small concrete cell. Never has he been so ashamed and remorseful. He is forced to call his father, who calls a lawyer. Within three hours, bail is set and paid and he is free to go but the event lingers.

"These things happen, Anil," his father consoles. "You're still newly married. A marriage is like a shoe. It gives lots of blisters at first but in time becomes wearable."

"And your wife," his father continues, "she's a traditional woman and knows how a good wife behaves. She'll say nothing and you'll be able to put all of this behind you."

But as good a traditional woman as Tanushri may be, and as ashamed as she is in having to relate even the most banal events of her personal life to a stranger, she is so deprived of warmth and so starved for the feminine voices of her mother, aunts and sisters that she is completely engulfed by the compassionate words of the hospital counsellor, who encourages her to only return home long enough to collect her and Tejas's belongings and leave.

Tanushri's nostrils are packed with cotton and her nose is the size of a turnip. Her head throbs and she finds it difficult to think. If she could think, all that would be humming in her head would be the static line of a dead heart—like the one she saw on a hospital monitor when she was admitted to Emergency. She cannot consider what she is doing. She allows the hospital counsellor to take Tejas, and a policewoman escorts her home.

"I need to speak to my wife alone," Anil demands, but the policewoman will not allow it.

"Tanushri," he shouts from across the room. "We need to work our differences out together, not with an outsider interfering. Please," he begs, his voice cracking like the hard shell of a nut.

What Tanushri does is disgraceful; it will lead to her censure. Her husband and his family will disown her, but she cannot stop herself. In her state of trauma, every woman's utterance evokes the authority of her mother, and the policewoman is telling her to ignore Anil, to pack her things, to move quickly, so she does not succumb to his words.

She throws her daughter's diapers, clothes and toys into a large green garbage bag, then begins to collect her own possessions. For the first time since Tejas's birth, she recalls the meat bones that still reside beneath the bed and, embarrassed for her forgetfulness as well as for her failure to bear a son, she tosses them quickly in among her belongings, promising herself to discard them as soon as possible.

The shelter she is taken to is a large grey, characterless building with an elaborate security system that renders it as intimidating as a penitentiary. Tanushri cannot see inside. Bright sunlight ricochets off its windows. They are all made of mirrored, bulletproof glass, and later she discovers they are sealed shut and rigged with an alarm that will produce a deafening screech if tampered with. Outside, under the awnings, two hidden cameras track passing movements. There is an armed security guard at the door and another in a booth full of screens who monitors every area of the building.

There are electronic doors that slide open and shut. From the inside, Tanushri can see everything that is happening in the street. She sees a man reading a newspaper as he waits for the lights to change, and a woman in a tight skirt and high-heeled shoes tottering out into the traffic, trying to hail a cab. The man unselfconsciously scratches his bottom. The woman keeps patting her windswept hair. This must be what it's like to be invisible, Tanushri thinks—to observe others without being observed—and she wonders if her mother might be watching her from some ethereal vantage and if so, what she must be thinking.

Tanushri already regrets coming here. It is like the severing of a limb. It can never be undone. There will always be a hideous scar, a defect. Tanushri puts Tejas down. The baby toddles to the doors and hits them with her tiny fists. The floor is polished tile and Tejas is wearing her first pair of walking shoes. Everywhere she goes the heels of her shoes leave thin black streaks. Tanushri apologizes to the security guard. She apologizes to the no-nonsense woman who arrives to be her guide at the shelter. "I will clean the floor," Tanushri offers, tears brimming.

The woman tells Tanushri not to worry and takes her to her room. It is small, carpeted and cozy. There's a flowered bedspread on the bed and ruffled curtains on the windows. There's a dresser, a desk, a crib and a changing table. Beside the bed are a nightstand and a lamp. Although her guide calls it "basic," Tanushri thinks it's very nice.

"Everyone cooks together," the woman explains, taking her along to the communal kitchen, "but you'll find out more about that tonight," she adds. Tanushri can barely suppress her sudden joy—women preparing meals together—just like in her childhood home, with her aunts and mother and grandmother all talking together, and she and her sisters, each assigned a task, taking the world in through the women's words. But this is not the situation at all. It is all very shameful and different now and the joy evaporates.

There is a common room in the shelter where the women and their children converge in the evenings to watch TV, listen to music and play cards. On the floor above, there are rooms where workshops on self-esteem, assertiveness, legal issues, and parenting, are conducted. "There are also lots of fun activities," the woman tells her, "like jewellery making and Latin dancing. Last week there was a fashion show—'Dressing on a shoestring.' It's too bad you missed it."

Tejas struggles out of her mother's arms and runs to a room she has spotted full of toys and children. It's a daycare and the woman tells Tanushri if she attends a workshop or needs to go out for an appointment at any time, she can leave Tejas there for free. Tanushri has never left Tejas with anyone but the hospital counsellor, and doesn't know how she will cope with such freedom. She feels again a sudden rush of joy, as if her life were beginning, as if the prospects of a future were spilling out before her, like a litter of stars or the colourful toys that attract Tejas, but she quells the feeling, for she knows in fact there is no light and colour. There is only darkness. Her life is ending. She has made a choice with irrevocable consequences and destroyed herself as certainly as if she had plunged a dagger into her heart.

Back in her room, she tries to absorb the full impact of her actions, but she is uncertain what the full impact will be. Thoughts burst into her mind like bubbles on a pot of soup. Even if Anil would take her back, could she ever overcome her shame? She begins to disperse the contents of her garbage bag, putting underwear in the dresser, hanging a blouse in the closet. She gives Tejas her favourite toy, a stuffed monkey that's been gnawed almost unrecognizable, but Tejas abandons it in favour of the sack of bones, which she finds on her mother's bed.

A tall lean woman, dressed in a tank top and cotton turquoise skirt, appears at the door. Her name is Melanie and she has a room across the corridor. "I see you have the same designer luggage I have," she says lightly, pointing at the garbage bag.

There is such humiliation in what has happened—so much disgrace. Laughter cannot possibly be appropriate here, Tanushri thinks, and now, to make matters worse, Tejas has dragged the sack of bones under the desk, opened it and dispersed the contents on the floor. Drool is dripping from her chin, pooling like syrup on the carpet as she gnaws on one of them.

"Is that your ex?" Melanie asks, regarding the bones.

Tanushri doesn't like this woman who invades her solitude and makes light of her misery. She is lacking proper reserve and it's as if she's mocking her.

"Give me that bone!" Tanushri demands and Tejas howls as Tanushri wrestles it free.

"Your baby looks forceful," Melanie offers. "Is it a boy or girl?"

"Girl," she murmurs. Even now, Tanushri feels degradation in announcing the gender of her child.

This is not the only time Melanie has been in this shelter. Her partner cracked three of her ribs, fractured her pelvis and broke her wrist the first time, but she went back. Six months later, she was in the shelter again—this time with a punctured lung and a knife wound in her chest.

Tanushri, embarrassed by this intimate and unsolicited confession, doesn't know what to say.

"I was looking at my body from the ceiling," Melanie tells her, "seeing the blood, watching the doctors work on it, knowing I had to crawl back in there somehow, even though it hurt so much."

There are things that ought not to be spoken, things that one bears in isolation and anonymity, Tanushri thinks, collecting the bones strewn across the floor. She is relieved Melanie has finished her story—relieved her own story hasn't come bubbling out. The bones are like heavy blocks in her hands and she wants to be rid of them, but the presence of this shocking woman prevents Tanushri from throwing them away.

The bones are so white and clean; they fit so neatly into the cloth sack Tanushri made that Melanie assumes it's a game. That evening when Tanushri sits at the large dining table, self-conscious and remote, sharing only the rice and vegetables the women have prepared, Melanie describes Tanushri's game and suggests she might teach them all to play. She does it as a kindness, to help bring Tanushri out of herself, to offer her a way into this community of women, but the kindness is not appreciated. Heat rises in Tanushri's cheeks. She knows she can never tell these women the truth of it, and so she lies. "It was my mother's game. I never learned to play it, myself."

A quiet voice at the end of the table emerges and dumbfounds Tanushri.

"I know the game. It's called the bone game. I can teach it." The woman who has spoken is Janet. She has a reputation for being both aloof and mysterious, a woman who does not often speak. Her room is a place of refuge for things of the natural world: the branch of a yew tree, the pelt of a fox, stones, shells and seeds. Above her bed hangs a shield she's made from a disk of redwood, an eagle's claw and an owl feather. She also wears an owl feather around her neck.

Melanie is the first to express enthusiasm at the prospects of learning a new game.

"Is it anything like mah-jong?" a woman inquires.

"Can you play it for money?" another asks.

Soon every woman at the table is talking about the game, while Tanushri just wants to shrink away.

"We've played bingo and bridge and gin rummy," Melanie says, "but the bone game!" It's as if she's speaking directly to Tanushri, although she is addressing the entire table.

They ask her to deliver the bones and Tanushri isn't strong enough to refuse. She feels there's nothing else she can do. If only she'd left them under the bed or disposed of them earlier. If only she'd known beforehand that her mother's instructions wouldn't work. She lifts Tejas from her high chair and takes her to their room. Perhaps if she tells the women the bones are gone, that she's misplaced them, perhaps they'll just forget. But before she has a chance to formulate a speech, Melanie is at her door, and Tejas has pulled the sack of bones from a drawer. "That kid of yours is brilliant," Melanie says.

The dishes have been cleared and washed, and the bones are set out on the dining room table for Janet to inspect. Her eyes are like light pools as they scan the bones. Tanushri holds her breath, wondering if Janet will announce her fraudulence, if she'll say, "These are just ordinary meat bones." But Janet begins to speak to the bones, then carefully divides the collection, putting the four small bones in one group and the eleven long bones in another. She removes a marker from her pocket and draws a circle around the circumference of two of the smaller bones.

"The one with the markings are the female bones and the ones without are the male bones," she explains.

Tanushri wants to stop her. To tell the gathering that Janet's lying. To explain. But she doesn't really want to explain—she can't explain—and so she stands mutely as Janet proceeds.

The women line two rows of chairs facing each other and divide into teams as Janet directs. Each team picks a leader and each leader is given a pair of bones, which they will hide in their hands and pass to other players. "The object of the game," Janet explains, "is to intuit where the female bones are hidden."

"A guessing game?" one of the women asks.

"No. More than that," Janet says.

Tanushri is appalled by Janet's barefaced lies, affronted by the smoothness and inventiveness of her deception. It is as if the blood in Tanushri's veins is becoming hot, as if the pressure of holding her tongue, of not telling the truth, is causing a bodily fever. Tejas squirms in her arms, as if she too feels the uncomfortable heat and no longer can bear the closeness of her mother.

"Intuiting and guessing are not the same things," Janet tells the women, "but you'll see as we play."

A few of the women nod their heads, as if they find some kind of resonance in Janet's words, but Tanushri's head remains sullenly fixed. If only she could release her tongue's trigger.

"There is something about the power of the voice, as well," Janet says, startling Tanushri. "You need to sing in this game. A good song can help your team win."

The women want to know what kind of a song to sing, and Janet says that they ought to try an assortment, that they'll know when they've found the right one.

"That sounds like what my mother used to say about finding the right man!" a woman shouts.

"How about 'Row, row, row your boat?'" another offers.

"How about 'Find, find, find the bone?'" Melanie says.

A few women on Melanie's team begin to sing and others scramble to the chairs and join them as the bones are passed. Tejas sways back and forth to the rhythm, free from her mother's arms. The other team quickly arranges itself and starts to sing, "The foot bone's connected to the leg bone. ..."

Incoherent words explode from Tanushri's mouth, crackings and hissings, but no one can hear them above the din of women's voices that grow louder under the dissonant current of songs. Tanushri turns to Janet who is caught in the spirit of the music, her feet stamping the rhythm, the owl feather around her neck, ensnared by her voice, flaps as if it would fly off. Tanushri reaches for Tejas, who is dancing in rapturous abandon and slips from her hands as if they had no substance at all. And then it is as if Tanushri is surveying the room from a great distance, as if she has lost her body completely to the incessant pulse below, but can see with a piercing clarity everything that has ever evaded her.

Her life spreads out before her, disjointed, fractured and in need of repair, but she sees how this might be done now. Her life with Anil seems to have existed a hundred years ago and like the bones her mother insisted she collect, was only as a means to this end—an ending, like all endings, that is fixed in the silent contracts of one's life, and can never truly be anticipated.

It is her mother, speaking through Janet, who brings Tanushri back to her body: she is telling her to find the female bones. And as clearly as she sees her mother, sisters, aunts and daughter extending before and beyond her into the past and future, she sees the hands that hold the female bones and begins to laugh. Her laughter and the voices of women rise like owls' wings, beyond the secure confines of the shelter, and out into the bright, star-filled night.

Maeengan Linklater

MOTHER EARTH

I'm an Indian
trying to wrap his braids
around Portage and Main
Winnipeg, Manitoba
I stand at the corner
the wind blows my hair
whipping strands like a hurricane
I'm blinded
by the sun reflecting
off the windows of buildings
scraping jagged scars
into the sky
bleeding down
to the sidewalk
I fall to my knees
place my ear on cement
trying to hear
your heartbeat
instead
I hear
steel pipes clanging
hissing
digging their claws
penetrating deeper
releasing
sewage
into your skin
unseen
ignored
by white eyeballs
who look at you
as an Indian prostitute

willing to go down
for twenty bucks a hit
I want to hold you
in my arms
allow my body
turn to dust
letting wild wind
carry my remains
like dandelion seeds
unto the Earth
but, there is this city
crawling
over your skin
disallowing you
fresh air
to breathe
disallowing you
sunlight
and honey brown skin
if I could
I would take you back
where you belong
in legends passed
around a winter's fire
I would take you back
where you would be free
to lay underneath stars
and northern lights
I would take you back
where you would be loved
for the nourishment you give
celebrated for each birth
that happens in spring
Mother Earth
I love you

Jackie Gay

THE WORLD FOR A GIRL

"What's it like round 'ere, then?" she said.

I hitched my shoulders. "'S okay," I said, glancing upstream, downstream, across to the spire of Newnham Church. Fishermen stood rooted in the river, up to their waists. A breeze snaked around us. I'd been staring at the old working barges stranded on the mud, deep into living on one, like Jane in *The Water Gypsies*, her first love—the wide, flowing river—sidelined by the dizzying kiss of the artist Mr. Bryan.

"The river's the best bit," I said.

She looked around too and I ran my eyes over her, the new girl, Donna, with purple hair like a crested grebe, black clothes and fingernails. The badges on her old man's jacket: The Clash, CND, a women's symbol. "You don't get many of them to the pound," Dad said, when he saw her for the first time scuffing around the village, squinting up the road as if a bus might appear.

Robbie and I glanced at each other, then Dad, then our eyes went back to the new girl in the street.

A branch snagged with spiky thorns drifted past. It was the scaly back of a river creature, the crest on the head of a monster. On the far bank, a giant slept, laid across the landscape, the autumn trees his beard, the overlapping hills his intertwined fingers.

"I'm gonna get a band together," she said. "Gorra do summat." Her accent was thick, intriguing. "Yow play?"

"Robbie's got a bass," I said. "My brother. Where are you from, anyway?"

"Dudley," she said. "The Black Country." Like your clothes, I thought. Then she jumped up. "Come over, at the weekend. Both of youm." And she was back on her bicycle, gone in a spray of gravel and a whisk of black and purple.

On the way back I looked at what it was like. Saul, my village, sits in the centre of the river's horseshoe bend and the land behind us, to Arlingham—where I was sitting when she came along—I've always thought of as mine. Robbie and I know every track, every ditch; the hedgerows, trees, streams and gullies. We could run tours, the scars on our bodies as waypoints. That's where Robbie bust his arm sledging (he has two neat pin marks), where I sliced the arch of my foot on a nail that poked out from the river's smooth bed (a ragged white *z*). That's the tree I fell from (a cartoon bump), the giant hogweed that blistered Robbie. I was heading straight home, I really was, but then I stood for a while and swerved across the marshy fields to catch one last glimpse of the river. Its movements called me—the pull of the tide, the sun captured by flowing wavelets, gold like Rapunzel's hair—and wiped out my resolve to study, be good, stop asking, to come home before dark. Birds clucked and chuckled above me, my feet swished through the glittering grass. I came out at the river and watched her curl and pulse. Then suddenly a swirling gathered and there was this great big *whoosh* and out of her rose a mud-green beast, grunting and spurting water from his beard-y mouth.

"Hello, Jennifer."

Bang bang went my icy heart.

"Cat got your tongue?"

Oh for God's sake, it was just Mr. Wilson, he knows my dad from fishing, lost his net, he said, had to go diving to fetch it.

"Like the river, don't you?" he said. "You're down here all the time."

What's it to you? I thought.

"He's always been a skin-flint," said Dad when I told him. "I'll have him over that one."

In the bath I sneaked a glance at my nipples, rolled my body so the water flowed over their tips. I watched my soapy hand ease towards one. My hips rose up from the foam, making ripples, making waves. I closed my eyes and let my hand stroke my thigh, edging inwards, felt my body filling up with heat. I have hairs down there now, a few more every week, and already I can't remember being hairless or when I first noticed I wasn't. The changes happened slowly but still caught me unawares—the bristles of my hairbrush grazing my breasts; my hand seeking Darren's skin through his shirt as we necked under the dripping horse chestnuts. "Can I do that?" he murmured and I flushed all over. I don't want him to ask me but I want him to want to just as much as I wished I could slide my hand further in, till it brushed me softly, like the wind does the hair on my head.

"Jennifer! Other people need to use the bathroom, you know. And I asked you clear up the table."

The water bucked as I came back round.

"Sorry, Mum." I scrambled out of the bath and rubbed myself down quickly, glad to be distracted from thoughts of bodies and boys and what you should and shouldn't feel and do. Would I be like this forever now? I thought, remembering me and Robbie not so long ago, swimming in the river, arms poised to dive, piercing the water through the floating ring, toes in the clay-like silt. The memories are kingfisher bright. Was *this*—the stiff nap of the towel down there—what would hijack my mind, now?

My little sister Katie was drawing horse heads in her scrapbook. They're all over the house—on the way up the stairs, on walls and windows, she draws them in the steam on the mirror in the bathroom, makes horse-head shapes with her peas and beans. I was like that with dogs. After clearing up, I grabbed Rolf and hauled him out into the street. Donna was there, lurking under my lamppost.

"'Ad to gerrout," she said. "Our Jimmie's gorra a girl round and they've gone all smoochy."

"Jimmie?" I said.

"Me brother. Mom's out and they doe want me hanging about the place."

A song was leaking from an upstairs window. "Don't take away… the music," and she cocked her head between "away" and "the music," a twisted expression on her face that said "soppy crap." The music hooked something in me though, just like the river does, my hips moving like I'd thought about with Darren but couldn't 'cause he's the boy next door, and then her front door opened and there he was. The one I had imagined pushing into, that I'd seen driving past in his van as I stood in my school socks and duffle coat at the bus stop. Lolling there, a hand's worth of skin between his jeans and T-shirt. "Comin' in, girls?"

Donna scowled. "Thinks he's God's gift," she said. "Come on, yow know this place. Where can we go?"

I looked up and there it was, the moon sliding out from behind a cloud. "To the river," I said.

It took us a while but I wanted to get to the exact right spot. We sat down; the river slipped silently below us. There was a splash somewhere near. Light rain was falling but we couldn't see it in the dusk, only feel it. I wondered if she felt it—she seemed like the kind of girl who could walk straight through thunder without a flinch.

"They can't make me stay 'ere. Mother thinks, 'She's skint, she can't go nowhere' but I can hitch, see. Em, my mate back 'ome, she hitches everywhere. Over to France, even. She's over there now, should a gone with 'er, I should. Soon as she writes I'll be off. I ent staying in a place called Saul for no bugger."

"What about your brother?" I said.

"He don't care where 'e is. Gets by on his looks, that one."

He *is* good-looking. Like James Dean or Elvis. I sneaked a glance at Donna in the dusk and she had the same square face and stand-up hair and black eyebrows. They were perfectly shaped, like they'd been painted on and for a second it was *his* face so close to me and I felt giddy, sick-hot.

"If she thinks bringing me 'ere is gonna save me she's got another thing comin'."

"Save you?" I said.

"There!" she said, jabbing the soil with a stick. "*You* gerrit."

I was wondering what it was that I understood when I heard it. A muffled roar, creeping closer. We could both hear it. She perked up, looked round, just like the woodpeckers and hares and even the fish underwater were, now it was coming.

"What is it?" she said, and it thrilled me that she felt the change as the tide flooded up the Severn and pushed into the narrow channel, building to a head, foaming and roaring.

"The Bore," I said. "Tidal waves in the river. People surf them."

She looked at me like I was mad—surfing, here in Gloucestershire—but it was true, though not at night. Only a crazy would surf in the dark.

"There's a big one predicted. Come on."

I grabbed her hand and ran, splashing through the fields, imagining the wave of mice and voles and rabbits moving with us. Badgers, deer—I know where they all live. A tide of mammals swept up in front of the oncoming waves, while seagulls danced above them. She was laughing as we scrambled along, the water rising with us, up to Framilode and we teetered on the wall as the waves crashed around us. When it was past, there was a glassy silence, the swollen waters pooling and hissing, the backwash slapping the banks. She went to speak but I stopped her, a finger on her lips. That's the best bit, the aftermath, feeling the water spread and settle, foam sizzling on the surface.

Some of the girls at school talk to their mums about sex but we're not that kind of family. Mum gave Robbie some leaflets (I found them in the airing cupboard) and asked me, hurriedly, if I knew the "facts of life." I nodded and that was that, even though the "facts" were from juniors and all I've had since are biology lessons on animal reproduction, which I don't need. Living here, you can't move for animals at it. I've read stories of course, which never give details, and then there's the songs, of infernos and blowing your mind. I heard them as I passed Donna and Jimmie's house, the music scooping my insides, making me feel a bit crazy. I walked Rolf in a circle around the village and the crooning followed me, breathy voices, curling on the wind.

"Anyone in there?"

I was still inside the music, picturing *him* heading towards me, smiling his sneaky smile. "Will it come again tonight?" Donna said.

"No, that's it for a month."

"What, like your periods?"

That was obvious once she'd mentioned it and I was embarrassed I hadn't worked it out before.

"Yeah," I said. "It's to do with the moon. When the tide's high at Sharpness, the Bore comes up here."

"That's why I could feel it then."

She seemed to be making some connection but I've always felt it coming, living so close. When I was little I'd lie in bed and hear the tumble of water and dream I was riding the swollen waves. Then Dad woke us early one morning and said, "Get your wellies," and we tramped out across the fields in single file to Overton where the estuary narrows and watched the white horses emerge from the grey dawn. Dad set off, running, running faster than we could to catch it as it hooked round the Horseshoe Bend. It was gone—the tail of the horse vanishing round the next loop of the river—by the time we caught up, Dad had to carry me home, sobbing, but I never missed it again. The next time I made sure I ran faster.

One day, Dad said the Bore might break right through, crash down on top of Saul. Imagine that, he said as I clung to his shoulder, imagining.

"Let's go to mine," said Donna. "They'm all out."

It was hot in their house and the living room was strewn with records. Donna slipped her hand inside her coat and pulled out a photo of another girl in black, aloof-looking, fierce. "This is Em," she said. "We were like that." She crossed her fingers on both hands.

"Has she rung you?"

She didn't answer. The front door clicked and it was *him*, swerving into the room, sweeping up a pile of albums, flashing a wolfish smile at me. Then Donna burst out. "I ent surprised, mind. I wouldn't write if I was 'er, the bollocking our mom giv 'er. As if upping sticks and dragging me down here is gunna reform me."

"But why do you need reforming?" I said, thinking it might be her clothes, the goth thing. She stopped her circuit round the room and looked at me, reached out and touched my cheek. A lock of her fringe wavered in the gas fire's draft. Then she laughed. "I don't," she said. "Hang on, I'll mek us a brew."

I could hear Jimmie moving around upstairs and that made me even hotter and I had to go and open the front door and gulp the damp air. "Are you OK?" she said, handing me a can of lager instead of a cuppa and I gulped at it greedily. "Drink, don't think," she said and before long we were giggling and snorting our way through a whole six-pack. Music wound down the stairs.

Put your body close to mine.

You're the one that I've been waiting for forever.

And Donna hooked her arm round my waist and pulled me round the room, pouting and mock-kissing the air, but in my head it was real. Her square face was his and the sighs were mine as the bliss spread out all around me.

The next morning I was woken by a rap on the front door. Half ten? I lay there, head throbbing, feeling shrivelled. I stank, too, like the gas that lives under the mud.

The thought that it might be Darren dragged me out of bed. I was supposed to meet up with him the night before.

I stumbled down the stairs and pulled on the front door, peering blearily through my fringe.

Standing there were Mr. Wilson and his creepy sons (Twins. They finish each other's sentences.) and the green of their fishing kit set off a nauseous wave. I lurched away, my duvet trailing, and then to make it even worse Darren walked past, firing me a murderous glance. "Dad's not here," I managed, closing the door and leaning on it, hot again, sweating. I saw me in the mirror, in my vest and knickers, a bruise of mascara smeared down my cheek, a hair or two snaking out down there.

I knocked on Darren's door. "Hey," I said.

"Remembered who I am then?"

"Darren, I'm sorry," I stuttered. "I only met up with Donna and we had a few drinks…"

"So," he said, folding his arms, "you stood me up for her."

I could easily have cried, him going all hard on me when it was just a stupid mistake. A month ago I'd have said, "Don't be a nob, Daz." But this heat in my body and Jimmie's wolfish looks and the blurring of Donna's face stopped me. I mean, he has got reasons.

"Are we still friends?" I asked, and I saw him sag but he hardened up again and half-closed the door.

"You were half-dressed," he said. "In the street for everyone to see."

"I don't know what's happened to you," said Mum.

"Carry on like this and you'll end up in trouble," said Dad.

They don't drink and we're not supposed too. Robbie said there was an almighty row when I got home, the worse ever by miles, and that Dad called me a strumpet. We're not that sort of family either.

I was banned from seeing Donna but worse than that, I had to stay in. Stuck up in my room with Robbie next door thudding away on his bass, I smouldered with more than just heat. I wasn't "in the street" for starters and I never asked for any of this. Running through the woods, feeling for secret handholds as I climbed the shadowed trees, watching the heron poised by the glassy canal as the mist clung to the water. That was my life and my land and my river and, lately, the only thing that could cool my smoking skin.

To their faces I was penitent. I played with Katie, helped round the house but it was no conversion. I "ent no Paul," as Donna would say. Robbie watched me; he knew. It was him that smuggled me the note.

We met at The Old Passage Inn. Donna had a pirate scarf round her neck, skull and crossbones, and we felt like smugglers, hugging the bushes away from the moonlight as we made our way down the riverside path.

"How d'yer gerrout?" she said.

"Through the window."

"Classic," she laughed, then, "*Shussh!*"

There was someone coming towards us, we pulled up our hoods and hunkered down. An old bloke with a skeleton bike, sniffing the air like a fox, looking over the river. A Bore watcher, too. He squelched on, tires hissing. I shivered and Donna squeezed my arm. "Ta for coming," she said. "I ent half missed yer."

"Did you hear from Em?" I said.

She turned towards me, face white in the frame of her hood. I saw the puffiness, heard the cracks as they spread through her voice. "She day want to know, Jen, I managed to gerrer on the phone but hers gone all cold. Like there's this *film* around her, worri cor get through." Just like Darren, sealing up like you're nothing to them and then Donna was crying, sobbing. The oncoming Bore rumbled, I could feel it building, rising in me like the heat. Donna was laugh-sobbing and clinging to my shoulders. She slipped (accidentally?) and our faces came close and she reached up, her lips on top of mine, working. I could taste her tears, the river's diluted saltiness. The Bore powered up, pushing on past as she pushed into me. Out at sea the tide reached its height. It held, for a moment, then turned, silently. After a while so did I.

Donna choked. "Sorry," I said.

"Yeah. Well. See yer, Jen." She released me and was gone. The church bells chimed to mark the passing of the Bore.

I should have followed, laughed it off, maybe even kissed her back but the moment had gone. I was too clumsy, like with Darren, I baited but then held back, sent signals and tried to erase them. So I took off sideways. Soaked through and crying too, up to my knees in bog then to my waist in ditch, I didn't care, I just ploughed on, dousing myself of her face and his. In my head, I could feel her lips, still, made them his, sank into the earth with his arms around me, at it like rabbits, like rams. Then the hissing, the glassy silence. A field, a ditch, the sky, but which field? The trees were unfamiliar, the moon was shrouded by clouds.

You'll end up in trouble, my girl.

Someone was near. I was suddenly alert, throat thudding, eyes darting this way and that. I'd been followed—I knew it instantly. We'd been followed, me and Donna, but he'd left her alone for me.

"Cat got your tongue?" he said.

"You've been wanting this, haven't you?" he said.

I can still hear him, feel the grip of his hand on my arm, smell his fishiness. The ground came up to meet me; roots wound around my waist. I tried to kick but my limbs were leaden, frozen. Did he know that? Did he wait? Picking me off then running me down.

Afterwards he pressed his finger on my lips, hard. Saliva curled in the back of my throat. I heaved myself up from the shape of my body pressed in the soil, pulled myself away from his handprints and boot marks. "You girls," he said. "Think the planet's all yours, don't you? A man's out here for a bit of fishing and then you come along with your dirty glances, sneaking out of your bedroom, running round all dishevelled like you do. ..."

He's Dad's friend; runs neighbourhood watch. I opened the door to him wearing my knickers. There in the field I could see my reflection then: the slipped-out hairs, his eyes tracing down me.

It's the look of distaste on his face that I can't wipe out, him looking down, on me. I loped home, hid my muddy clothes, pulled the sheets up, hugged my knees there under the window with its horsehead stencil, gritty and frozen till dawn. When I dared run a bath I lay in the boiling water, cold as a slab of meat, my nipples flaccid and a spike of ice between my legs.

"Jenny," says Mum, tapping on my door. "You're allowed downstairs, you know."

"We could go for a bike ride," says Dad at dinner. "I know you've missed going out but you do have to learn, Jennifer."

I chew and chew but the food stays solid.

"Sis," hisses Robbie as I'm waiting for the kettle. "I can pass a note back to Donna if you want."

In my room I pull down my posters of Dexys and Kenny Dalglish. Under my bed are the old ones, from when I was little: "English hunting dogs," "Trees of Britain" and a map of the world with explorers' routes with square-rigged ships meeting spouting whales, islands of seals, and polar bears hunting. "There be monsters," it read in old-world script. When the gravel hits my window I freeze again but it's Donna, hissing up at me. "Jen! Come down, we're still mates ent we? Yer mom and dad are out, I just sin 'em go."

I run down and let her in—don't care what they say—because I know how it happened, that I, too, would have made myself slip, closed my mouth on Jimmie's. Tried. The heat's all gone, now. Mum and Dad should be pleased. Donna's face is sagging with guilt and sorrow and I say, "No, no, no, Donna it's not that, it really isn't."

"So worrever's the matter?" she says.

My blood drains away. I feel it pooling. Can't even think the words. "What, Jenny?" she says, reaching for my hands, rubbing them in hers like she knows that I'm cold.

"Do you know Mr. Wilson?" I say and she shudders.

"Creep," she says. "Stay away from him."

I start to quiver, like a leaf in the wind, the last leaf on a branch. "Oh my God," she says, her voice thicker than ever, curdling. "What's the man done? What has he done to you, baby?"

I look in her eyes and I see.

She knows. Donna knows what it's like around here.

What the world can be like for a girl.

She says I should tell. But she won't make me. I love her for that and I tell her. "You love our Jimmie more," she says. I'm so grateful for her teasing that I cry all over again.

Donna told him she knows. In his ear as he fished, like a djinn. "You're rumbled, pal. It's over." I'm in awe of her guts. "It's youm that'll have to be brave," she says. "Cos hims done this before, I know it. He'll do it again, Jen."

I'm cold. I hardly sleep. Instead I look out at the silvered fields, feel the pulse of the river behind them. I think of the people who surf on the Bore, how I watched them, back then in the used-to-be. Gliding past the wind-brushed fields, arms spread, balanced. And I do want my fields back, my river, the body he pressed in the mud, and I cup that tiny flame. It's blue like gas and stutters at the slightest breeze.

My face is white as paper on the glass.

The whiteness moves through the watery fields. There are monsters underneath.

I can't go out there.

Only crazies go surfing in the dark.

"The World for a Girl" was first published in The Malahat Review, *no. 168*

Joanna Lilley

WE CAN BE ANYTHING

artist

Our mother melts margarine I'd drink
if she wasn't looking,
adds a crackle of brown sugar,
pours in a long, soft whisper of oats,
salted by slim fingers
I wish I'd inherited

When the flapjack has cooled as long
as it cooked, it's perfect
Eldest of four disordered sisters,
an octave older than me,
you should know this too

Our mother lays a tea towel
over the tray like a blanket over you
and takes the rest of us swimming
Returning, she lifts the tea towel,
self-taught magician, to reveal a silver square
and a diminishing daughter
with at least some food in her stomach

At supper, you fork, one-elbowed,
more to the floor than your mouth
Berated, you shriek back your chair,
race your rage upstairs
oblivious of our cigaretted mother
sitting plateless

At night you bind my hands in gauze and plaster,
until they're voluptuous
Mine are plaster casts of yours,

large-knuckled, double-jointed thumbs
but you've forgotten your own hands;
the wire is showing through
and you're the artist,
lines sharper than you can draw,
stomach scooped deeper than you can sculpt
I wish I could give you back my voluptuous hands

musician

We raise our hands out of the happy sea
and pour back more sparklings than a million gems
I drip onto a swelling notebook
while you practise your embouchure
until, bored with our Ionian paradise,
we make next summer's plans
How I'll join you on your bullion bridge
and we'll swim with seals

You picked considerately from the palette
our artless parents made us share
We can be anything as long as we're artists
If you can draw, we'll never know
but you play sweetly enough
to make us cry

Yet not enough to earn a living
Keeping your mouth full keeps you happy
and your mind off music
even if you do keep changing the recipe,
adding dates and nuts,
until you find a new religion
and lose your appetite

You were trying to understand
the sister between us
Seeking her truth, you found yours
I should have known you'd pass it down to me
If I hadn't taken it my hands
would have been free to break our mother's fall

dancer

Crushing chilblains into your blocks,
you point your toes and knees
and smile as if you know
compared to the pain to come,
this is nothing
There's silver inside your bones,
gold in your hair

You plastic-pant yourself,
shrink-wrap your hips,
choreograph yourself inside out
into a tiny sweated space

A tray of flapjack left to cool
you say it was our springing, splotchy dog
who licked it silver clean
You're better at maths than me
I never put two and two together
until you write a bile-scented letter
and deliver it to the kitchen table

Clasping a prayer of tea to cram your stomach
you kneel at the pantry door,
begging us not to unlock it
We take you where we can
tell everyone who thinks they know
Patient faces talk to you in small rooms
and us in corridors and, when you ask,
we unlock you, and tell you lies we mean

In a city by a sea,
other arms pull you up for air,
exchange Fonteyn for a past
you can spend the rest of your lives remembering
Of all of us, I thought it would be you
who would have our mother's hands

writer

Growing not up but sideways
I dodge the butts of your ready-steady palms
Youngest and smallest
I daren't grow higher than any of you
Largest and shortest
I eat as much as I can stomach
A tuberous, underground person
who burrowed so deep
I came up in another land

When I visit
I will make our mother flapjack
and hope I can remember
how to make it perfect

Elee Kraljii Gardiner

LIBRARY

I like to read
bodies
when women are naked
together. To take up the simple study
of a breast as she leans
to towel a foot, the weighted
silence hanging
as we take in
each other's shape.
To sense ourselves
unpeeled, shining.

In this classroom
lessons are
simple; the geometry
of scapulae, the centipede scar
ambling down one woman's spine,
or the scarred hollow
on a girl's arm
where the skin still pulls.

I find comfort
in the silver line riding low
on bellies around me, proof
that some have redoubled ourselves
through pain.
I too have a belly graffitied
in lemon juice lines.

Most are busy
with their trappings as I step
from the shower, decked in droplets,

yet one woman inclines
her head, as if to say
I know how it is,
and this is some peaceful heaven.

Among us
are women inscribed
with a blue ink
I can't translate.
What to make of the ribbon
penned "For Steve"
above the crevice of her buttocks?
Or the rash of identical
sunbursts resembling messy gunshots
on four calves in this one room.
There is enough violence
around our bodies
without writing it deep
but I keep silent and offer my body
to those who would read it,
those who might need it to know
that every skin is marked.

Caitlin Ross

BLINDERS

At school there's a girl nobody knows. We've seen her around, obviously; you can't walk up and down the halls of a middle school looking like her and not get noticed. This girl is marshmallow limbs stuck onto an aggressively plump torso, topped off with a thick helmet of tightly wound curls and frizz. Her pale skin is a vibrant white reminder that she probably never has a reason to go outside. It's not like other kids show up at her house and beg her to come out and play. Twelve years spent indoors has left her skin a pure white canvas upon which every moment of shame and embarrassment shows up as forcefully as a drop of fresh red paint. To make matters worse, she wears tight little shorts that ride up those thick white thighs, and sweatshirts covered in pictures of stallions charging through rivers and lone wolves howling at harvest moons. So yeah, we notice her, but no one ever talks to her.

Other awkward kids walk these halls: kids who tuck their sweatpants into their socks, who pee their pants in front of their whole English class, who smell like tuna every day of the week. The difference is that these kids manage to find each other and band together in the face of the unforgiving prepubescent awkward stage that they hope to one day outgrow. When the teacher announces a group project, the kid who tucks his sweatpants into his socks and the girl who smells like tuna automatically lock eyes. They know they're going to work together and if the kid who peed his pants in English class ends up without a partner, he, too, will be allowed to join their group. They all bear some unforgivable black mark on their social transcript and they become friends out of necessity.

But this one girl, she's different from them. She must be in special ed because I've never had a class with her and neither has anyone I know. She never gets a chance to make friends—even out of necessity, because she's never around other kids. Sure, I see her in the hall between classes sometimes or waiting at the bus stop after school, but that's it. No group projects or team sports force us together, and despite a quiet but persistent voice in the back of my head telling me that this situation is somehow wrong, it's easier to just go on attending school not knowing this girl.

The system we've worked out (we ignore her, she ignores us) has worked just fine up until this year. Every September a new batch of kids graduates from the elementary school and joins us at middle school. Rather than just ignoring this remote peer, a few of the boys who arrived this year have chosen to pay extra attention to her. By extra attention, I don't mean that they eat lunch with her, invite her to sleepovers or arrange surprise birthday parties for her. By "extra attention" I mean that instead of having fun with her they have fun at her expense, and instead of learning her name they decided to make one up for her. This group of boys calls her the Albino Rhino.

These days when I walk to and from class I hear chanting from down the hall. "Albino Rhino! Albino Rhino! Albino Rhino!" The lilting melody of this chant is deceptively cheerful and, although I never join in the chanting, I sometimes find myself humming the tune under my breath before realizing what I'm doing. Unfortunately, the name and the chant are catching on. I guess we never really had a reason or a way to talk about her before, but now that she has a name people are starting to tell stories.

I ask my younger brother, who is in the same grade as the boys who invented the name Albino Rhino, what he knows about this girl. "I don't really know her," he begins. I can tell that he's uncomfortable with the discussion. He too would rather not talk about her, or even know her, but it's becoming hard not to.

"I hear they call her The Albino Rhino," I say.

"Yeah," he replies. "I heard she charged at some guys the other day. Kind of like a rhino."

"Wow," I say. "That's kind of unfortunate, I guess."

"I know," he says. "It really is."

With that, the conversation is over. What else is there to say? Neither of us is comfortable with the name calling and bullying, which is rapidly becoming more and more accepted by the student body. At the same time, neither of us has the power to change it. I am a tomboy band geek who is on a first name basis with the school librarian because I've checked out so many books in the last three years, and my brother is in the middle of trying to recover from being an overweight kid with a mullet who wears flannel shirts and trainers by cutting his hair and joining the school basketball team. Neither of us can risk an alliance with the Albino Rhino. And even if we did, our solidarity wouldn't do much to change her social fate. Our silence is an unspoken agreement that we will try as hard as we can to go on pretending that she is just some girl, without a name, who nobody knows.

I haven't thought about this girl in days, except when I overhear some scrawny guy mouthing off to his buddies about how he "almost got charged by the Albino Rhino on the way to class." But today, leaving school a little later than everyone else after going to pick up my tenor saxophone from the band room, I hear a familiar chant, louder and more vicious than ever. "Albino Rhino! Albino Rhino! Albino Rhino!" I feel sick hearing the song and the shouting, even sicker when I hear the boys laughing. They sound like they're having fun.

I turn the corner from the cement bus compound onto a gravel path leading down to the main field, and what I see is impossible to ignore. A group of four boys have surrounded Albino Rhino on the field. They look like apes leaping around her in a circle, reaching down to pick up clumps of freshly mowed grass and throwing them at her. They seem to be trying to get the acid green grass clippings to stick to her helmet of frizzy curls. I walk down the gravel path, keeping a steady gaze on the savage ritual unfolding. One of the boys turns around, a heavy wad of grass clippings that reeks of hay fever and baseball games resting in his delicate pink palm. He makes eye contact with me, laughs cheerfully and throws the grass at the frozen Albino Rhino with extra force.

I put down my saxophone case and clench my sweaty hands into useless fists. "You guys are assholes!" I scream. "Leave her alone." They drop the grass clippings, much to my surprise, and actually do look a little ashamed.

"Jesus," said the tallest of the boys, "we were just—" He gets cut off when a clump of grass sails into the back of his head. The girl they call the Albino Rhino is shaking and shrieking, hurling grass clippings in every direction. Some of the grass is thrown towards me, although none of it actually hits me. She lets out one last terrified roar and races off the field, back towards the school. "That's what you get for trying to help the Albino Rhino," says the tall boy.

"Fuck you guys." I reply. "She has a name."

When I get home my mother asks me how my day at school was. "It *sucked*," I say, throwing my backpack and saxophone to the floor and stomping up the stairs to my room. I slam the door behind me and go straight to the bookshelf. I begin furiously tearing books from the shelf until I find my yearbook. I scan the pages, and there she is. Even on the page her mug shot stands out from the others.

The Albino Rhino: *Candace Bloom.*

Christin Geall

THEY LIKE TO WATCH

I've learned how to have sex online. First, I take my laptop to my bedroom. Then, I put on a suede black skirt and stockings that end in lace around my thighs. I start slow and work down. My camera doesn't zoom but I can move closer to it for detail, to show the curve of a hip or the pink of a lip. I can do angles and attitudes and orgasms. In fact, I could "do" almost anyone who cared to watch.

But I don't.

I strip and play with my lover who lives in another country. Three years ago, when we were living together for the first time, we never would have done this sort of thing. I didn't know it was so easy to have live video sex over the Internet. But three years ago my life changed when an ad from a porn site flashed over my boyfriend's email one night.

"What's that?" I asked. His computer was propped up on his lap, its screen facing me.

"Spam," he said.

"I never get that stuff. Have you ever watched it?"

"No. But I get the emails."

Men, I've heard, are visual; they like to watch. They like landscapes, abstracts and panoramas of arched backs and raised rumps. They like views too—mirrors hung beside beds, angles to catch the movements of curves. Men, I've learned, like women in the light.

I go away for a week and return to find his email open, so, I spy. I see what I don't want to see: "Babes ready for action." I feel scared, but so what? It's junk mail. But why do my hands sweat? Why do I need to search the history and why do I find a thong site listed that he visited a few days ago? He must have been buying underwear for me. It's okay, I think, that's nice. But scrolling over the week of my absence, a freight train barrels into my chest because click after click after click tells me he lied.

I do this when I fall in love—stand naked in front of mirrors and smile. That winter before porn, before the fights, the crying and the anger, I had performed for my lover. I would watch my body like a dancer, see it move and lift, bend and become something different under his gaze. I let him look at me everywhere then, and the more he looked, the more he adored me and the more I loved him.

But the day I discovered Internet porn, I rubbed myself raw. I watched too, rapt and repulsed, and did the very thing that upset me the most about him—I had sex with pictures of strangers.

That night, trust flew out the door the minute I called him a liar. It left us with a shell of love, something fragile, sucked dry—a relic I refused to touch. I sat on his couch, but he could see I was gone from his bed, from his house, from his life.

He cried. Begged to explain. Said he shouldn't have lied. That nobody knew. It, he pleaded, had nothing to do with me.

It, I said, was over.

Alone in bed, miles away, I closed my eyes to replay the memories of our lovemaking in my mind. I saw him staring down at me, his eyes watching me, watching him, watching us. He would throw back his head and tell me I was beautiful in these scenes and I would yell for more of him, for more of his love.

But in the solitary darkness of an empty bed, the vision of his eyes made me ashamed. I hadn't realized then I'd been so exposed.

I felt I could not love a man who used online porn. It wasn't romantic; it was weird. My jealousy said he had given himself to other women, maybe even hundreds of them since we first began dating. I could not be those women, could not become a horny college girl, an Asian hottie or one with D-sized cups and pink lipstick. Nor could I have orgies, do other women, or even, for that fact, swallow. I, in short, felt I was not the only woman he wanted to watch.

Porn, I've since learned, is addictive. The Internet has sites called "no-porn," "pornfree" and "porn" anonymous to help the thirty million people who log on to porn sites every day. There are software systems, support groups and books people can read to help break the habit. But I didn't know this then. For all the porn sites I visited in those weeks after my discovery, I never once thought to type "porn addiction" into Google. I never once thought that my man had joined the millions that were hooked.

When we spoke next I accused him of having no imagination. He continued to plead that porn had nothing to do with me, that it was his problem and that he didn't want it in his life anymore, that he would get help. I said that he needed it. He said he needed me.

He told me this and I tried to believe him. I felt like I was sitting with an alcoholic, listening to answers and excuses for an addiction that he was not in control of. How could anyone with a sex life like ours need anything else? He said he'd never watched when I was around; he didn't need to. He'd started using porn the year before we met, when he'd been lonely, bored or anxious. He slipped back into it when I went away and once he started that week he couldn't stop. It was a quick fix, he said, but he felt perverted, dirty, and hated himself for watching. Yet he kept logging on because the only one he thought he was hurting was himself.

I remembered the girls then, the girls who looked lost, not found. Exploited girls who didn't look like happy exhibitionists; they looked trapped, in drugs or poverty, sadistic relationships and abusive situations. The fancy ones, the Jenna's and tame ladies, were trapped too—in expectations, cosmetic surgeries, reductions, enlargements, lipo, waxing, spray tanning and makeup. There was a cost to his actions in other words, a cost that affected me.

But making one man answer for the plight of women is never an easy place to start a discussion. Porn, its societal and personal implications were not topics he had considered. He did not think of those women as real women. He used them for what they offered and asked little more.

I felt like a proselytizer at this point, beating him up with arguments because I was hurt. I felt ugly and at the same time would say things like, "You just love me because I look like a porn star," which in a way, is true. He probably would have clicked on my description: *Lean, natural blond. Chesty, and well-proportioned. Lips, full. Eyes, green. Loves sex.* But this was no consolation. I despised myself for measuring myself against those women and I despised him for wanting them. Even once.

So we stared at each other between my diatribes, between his pleading and my silences. We felt estranged but we were not strangers to the intimacy born from talking about arousal. Sex, the topic we never wavered from in those weeks after the porn, was something we both now knew to be treacherous and therefore enticing.

It took weeks for me to kiss him and longer still for us to make love. When it finally happened, we cried in the dark. He promised me his faithfulness. I promised him I would try to forgive.

It wasn't easy. At bars, every woman in a push-up bra and tight low-rise jeans looked like a threat. Advertisements, commercials, movies, magazine covers, the Internet, email and even jokes reminded me how hard it was to operate in a world of images when the person you love once used them like a drug.

I restructured my time so we were not apart, so that he could not be tempted, and we acted differently in the bedroom too; we didn't play. Sex became serious, loaded and at the same time, even more important to our relationship.

But part of us hadn't changed. We wanted to see one another in the light. So we started making out in the bathroom again, near mirrors and on floors. It felt different and better and scary because I had to go away for six weeks.

I asked him how he'd do. He said he'd be fine; I didn't need to worry. I believed him, but I thought I could do this. Let's make a video, I said. He said, you're kidding.

It worked, for both of us—scenes for me, scenes for him. In the best scenes we laughed or pretended or forgot that both of us now were watching.

And yet, I don't know if I'm alright. I don't know if the DVD we made and the video "chatting" we now do proves desire can trump politics or if I've simply found some beauty in seeing all the parts of our history make up a whole new sexual relationship. Our online "porn" is not our mainstay; it's filler, dosed out over gaps in contact. We use it to quench the thirsts of separation, not to create more space between us.

I still know porn can hurt but people like Paris Hilton don't bother me so much any more. Paris is famous because of her porn, because raunch culture needed an icon to usher in the popular fashion of our age. Porn is what some young women do: they take pole-dancing classes to learn to act like strippers, do lap dances and kiss one another to attract the eyes of men—men who they know watch porn.

So now when I set up my camera, I see two frames; the small one nests inside the other. In one, I see the man I love, his hands, his body, his smile. I tell him how to move in that space, hear him say what he knows turns me on. In the other, I see myself—flushed, illicit, beautiful and open. I know it's not the real me, but it's still a part of me, that we both, now, watch.

A version of this essay appeared in Monday Magazine *in 2006*

Algebra Young

THE BOX

In the world of the construction industry you experience many things. There is always a sense of awe when you see the finished product, a brand new building standing where nothing more than a hole had been before, but there is so much more to the job than that. There is more to the job than the job. There are lunches and coffee breaks, there are smoke breaks, there's the afternoon drive, but most importantly of all, most essential to a person's survival, there is the potty break.

This week the construction site was flooded with a hundred new workers and the cheap-ass site supervisor decided to cut the number of porta-potties in half. And cutting the number by half, you discover, means from two down to one. You have had years of construction experience, but with over 130 men occupying the site this job is becoming a doozy. As you have learned from the past few weeks on the site, the potty is only emptied once weekly. Since the site's population has more than tripled you can only expect the worst.

In an effort to increase the number of johns on site, you remind the site super that if there is even one woman on the site, which you are, there is supposed to be a female-only toilet available. He tells you to go fuck yourself, but not in so many words. Though your co-workers are no different from any other contributing member of society, for some reason the moment they cross the threshold into this job site, they become some of the most unhygienic creatures ever considered human. Today you are one of the only women on site working with thirty carpenters, twenty electricians, ten plumbers and seventy brick layers, all of whom are men.

Approaching the porta-potty and anticipating the horrors about to unfold you prepare yourself by taking a few deep breaths. This helps give you minimum aerobic exposure to the plastic box from hell. If lucky and well-practised, you should be able to make it into the porta-potty, lock the door, have your pants down and be more than halfway through your bowel movement before the dreaded first breath.

Outside the door of the potty you are already feeling overwhelmed by the olfactory overload of impending despair. As you reach out to the off-white pull knob that will unlock the undisputed gate to hell, you begin to ask yourself if you really have to go that bad? If not, odds are you will turn around and march directly back into the loving bosom of the job site. You will cross your legs and eyes until the next break when you will rush off to the closest family restaurant and threaten to murder the first person to come between you and a human-waste receptacle of pretty much any kind. But odds are good that knowing what lies beyond the potty door and still putting down your tools, you really have to go.

With the deepest lungful of air you can muster, you fling open the door. A gust of warmth erupts from the box into the cold December day as the heat of the human waste contained within has been left to fester, incubating in its plastic shell. All of your senses jump to life. It is no longer only a smell. It is a taste. It is a feeling. It creeps up your face and into your ears where your nerves can be heard screaming for mercy. You spin to face the door and one hand pulls it shut behind you while the other hand is already fast at work on the fly of your pants. Your fingers are quick and nimble from mentally rehearsing on your trip to the box. You have your pants down in record speed and plop your rump quickly on the wet seat. Not moist but downright wet. Yes, in another situation you may have been disgusted by this and taken precautions to avoid such an unpleasant experience, but in the case of the job-site porta-potty, you thank your lucky stars that the urine from a handful of men is all you just sat in.

Until this point, you have simply been leaning forward pulling the door of the potty shut, but now you spare the half second to lock the door as this next step is the most challenging of all. Sacrificing this moment will be one of the wisest investments you could possibly make. The moment of truth.

Telling your sphincter to relax while the rest of your body is being informed that you are on the frontlines of your own personal judgement day is like giving a cat a bath: it ain't gonna happen. Luckily by this time, the neurons that have been reporting this sensory massacre have had their ends frayed into oblivion. This is good because it means you are able to concentrate less on the astronomical stench and more on controlling your bodily functions. As you begin to make progress, and right on cue, your lungs begin to sting and ache. The time for the first breath has come. Tears well in your eyes at the prospect of the unimaginable act you are about to carry out. Earning a few extra moments, you begin to exhale in the hopes that it will appease your rioting organs but to no avail. Trembling, you open your lips, and with a disgusting suck you pull the putrescent porta-potty gasses into your body.

This triggers an entirely new experience of sensory trauma as the flavour of the air brushes against your tongue. The experience is so agonizing your insides jump to life in an attempt to spring from the prison that is your body and make their way out of the potty on their own. Your eyes roll into the back of your head as nausea strikes your guts like a sledgehammer. Your one and only saving grace is the knowledge that if you are going to puke, you would have to do it directly into the hole. The threat of this fate somehow gives your mind the supernatural ability to deny your body its most basic functions, forcing it into submission once more. This has required so much effort and time that you must now take another breath.

This breath is easier than the last. The first breath is caked so thick to your mouth that the second is able to slide over it without too much destructive force (in the painting industry, we refer to this phenomenon as "build"). The poisonous gas rushes into your malnourished lungs, soothing them after the lengthy anaerobic trial. With that you take another breath and another until your insides are appeased. Granted, you won't be able to taste for a week, but at a time like this you are happy your body was designed to shut down your senses after an ordeal such as this.

As your body acclimatizes to this new harsh environment, you are able to relax and breathe easy. You begin to visually explore your surroundings to distract yourself from the ever embarrassing act you are presently engaged in.

You notice the urinal beside you. Odds are it is practically overflowing with the bodily fluids of what must be at least one hundred men. Though the urinal portion of the potty is designed to drain so as to avoid having a piping hot bowl of stagnant urine just hanging out, men have a tendency to want to aim at things while relieving themselves. This leads them to almost always target the small round sanitizing disk placed at the top of the urinal. As you can imagine, the thunderous torrent of urine repeatedly hitting the disk causes it to slip down the plastic until it is directly over top of the drain, plugging it completely. Never would any man take the initiative to get a stick or something to nudge the disk off, nor would he ever bother to pee in the toilet instead of the urinal unless it is absolutely overflowing (and then he would proceed to get it all over the seat when he finally does). The urinal just begins to fill up until you have at least two gallons of urine threatening to slosh out of the trough at the slightest movement. You may wonder why such an incredible design flaw is allowed to persist, but it is just one of the world's great mysteries.

Perhaps out of fear of queasiness, or just raw disgust, you try to turn your attention away from the massive bowl of manly essence beside you. Looking on the walls you discover a plethora of scribbles. The most obvious of these are the drawings. These consist largely of female genitalia. Extremely graphic portraits of vaginas are etched into the plastic with tools of all sorts: pencils, markers and blunt instruments like nails and screw drivers. While examining these portraits you may notice that though certain parts of the female anatomy have been given an attention to detail rivalling that of Michelangelo, other areas are certainly lacking. None of the women portrayed have heads, hands or feet. As a matter of fact, these dismembered torsos are lucky if they have much more than the absolute bare essential to constitute "spreading." Among the men on the site, there are many different kinds of artists. Some prefer the very geometric circle inside a circle to depict a breast, whereas others take much more intricate approaches to their work. Still more look like they tried to slap their picture on the wall while being chased down by the Vatican police.

The depiction of male sexual organs are scarce in obvious inverse proportion to the numerous homophobic comments on the walls. There's "you are gay," the "Steve and Dan are gay," and the always interesting gay checklist. For example, you are gay if: you are a carpenter, you are a fag, you watch *Grey's Anatomy*. Usually rather nonsensically, the terms "gay" and "fag" are peppered about the walls.

Another interesting example of porta-potty graffiti you may come across, should you be lucky, is the always enjoyable poetry and limericks. Old favourites can often be found:

There once was a man named Dave
who kept a dead hooker in his cave.
She smelled like shit and had only one tit,
but think of the money he saved.

There are also interesting original works such as:

Kissed my sweetheart, got erected.
Popped the question, was rejected.
Now I sit upon this seat,
smelling shit and beating meat.

And finally, a new and creative piece:

WCB Regulation 629.4: All turds longer than 8 inches must be
broken off and lowered by hand to avoid chemical splash.

Though at one point in your life you may have found these comments crude, offensive and downright revolting, life in the trades requires a thick skin and you must learn to laugh these things off.

As you finish your business you tidy up, taking more time to be hygienic now that you are desensitized to the effects of the porta-potty. As you leave a fellow worker asks, "How is the cone today?" The cone, of course, is when so much feces has built up that it actually begins to protrude up out of the bowl, causing the user to have to squat above the toilet in order to use it. As unpleasant an image as it is cones are all too common in the construction industry today.

"Not bad," you will reply, for today was one of those lucky days when there was almost no cone to speak of.

And with that, easily the worst part of your day out of the way, the day seems brighter. You head back to the job site eager to pick up your tools and forget the events of the past few minutes. Forget the ugliness of the box and look forward to making the world a slightly more beautiful place. Or at least a couple walls.

Andrea Routley

INTERROGATION

I had a feeling there was some sort of check-up I should get. That's why, when I was twenty-one, I went to see my mother's doctor—to ask her about this. I said exactly, "Is there some sort of annual check-up I should get?"

She gave me a physical: checked my heart with a stethoscope, my reflexes with a hammer and my breasts with her hands. I felt self-conscious—the deodorant under my arms had turned into powdery lines.

Three years later, I found out about pap smears and decided I should get one of those. I moved around a lot, so I had no regular doctor. I went to a walk-in clinic.

The carpet was grey and so flat it could be swept. The receptionist sat behind a high white counter so that only the top half of her head could be seen. I leaned over the counter to whisper the nature of my visit.

In the doctor's room there was one chair and a vinyl bed covered in tissue paper. I knew the doctor would sit in the chair, so I sat on the bed. The tissue paper crinkled under my butt. I sat carefully so I wouldn't tear it. On the counter across from me were a jar of cotton swabs and a tube of K-Y Jelly. On the wall, a poster illustrated the stages of fetal development.

The doctor entered and said hello without looking at me. He was a man, middle-aged, with dark brown hair parted on the side. He sat down and asked me what I wanted.

I told him: a pap smear, an STD test, a pregnancy test.

He told me there was no female doctor at the clinic. I said that's okay. I don't care. He asked me if I had a family doctor. I said no. He asked why. I said I moved around a lot. He said there's a new practice down the street and they might be taking patients. I said I'm just visiting my Dad and I want to get a pap smear today. He suggested the hospital. And that was it. That's why I never got the pap smear.

Next question: "Why do you want an STD test?"

My response: "Isn't it a good idea to get those once in a while?"

Next question: "Do you use condoms?"

My response: "Everybody knows to use condoms but it doesn't always happen."

Next question: "How many partners have you had?"

The bed felt like a table. The tissue paper was a petri dish. I was bacteria.

He took my blood and I peed in a cup. I dragged my feet over the grey carpet out of the office, into the sun. I felt weird. I sat down on the curb behind the clinic and cried. I started talking out loud, saying all the things the doctor only implied.

I will not give you a pap smear, a routine exam.

I don't want to spoil my afternoon by looking at your genitals.

What have you done to deserve an STD test? Are you a slut? Do you like it up the ass? Or are you just stupid?

Explain yourself.

Fiona Tinwei Lam

EXAMINATION

You are splayed like a specimen
under fluorescent lights,
the doctor's fingers rummaging in your body
as if it were a broken toaster.

You talk about who hurt you
to this white-coated confidant.
His metal tools aligned on a metal tray,
his hands glowing, opaquely unreal
in plastic gloves, his glances
of polite concern.

You hear waves of footsteps,
rattling stretchers and carts
wheeled on endless linoleum,
doctors being paged, someone crying
down a labyrinth of corridors,
all sounds swabbed
and wrapped in gauze.

An intern watches your unravelling,
his thoughts dammed against a smirk.
You feel your vulva turning
into pussy.

The fingers snag a nerve.
Your eyes shut. You know
theirs stay open.

"Examination" was previously published in Fiona's book, Intimate Distances
(Nightwood Editions)

Trysh Ashby-Rolls

UNBECOMING A PHYSICIAN

During the 1960s, in Swinging London attending theatre school, I was a dope-smoking, hard-drinking, sleeping-around party babe. That was until 1963, when I met a man in Spain who held me hostage for six weeks, repeatedly raping and torturing me. I tried to tell my mother what happened but she "didn't want to know," so I turned to a friend for help. Her father, a psychiatrist, referred me to another psychiatrist I dubbed Jumbo. In return for free sessions I lay on his couch, undid my blouse, let him fondle my breasts. Maybe more—I don't remember.

In 1971, married with a baby, I returned from a new home in Canada to confront him. "Sex came up. We dealt with it," he said, immediately pulling strings to commit me to the back ward of a mental hospital: a place where, diagnosed psychotic, I was stuffed with zombie-making pills, threatened with force-feeding and shock treatment. My world, its air reeking of unwashed humanity, urine and disinfectant, shrank to a space bordered by cracked walls, barred windows and multiple locked doors. There was no escape until a man in a white coat deemed me fit.

Deeply depressed, home in Toronto, I sought another psychiatrist. Bill prescribed mood-altering medications and recommended weekly psychotherapy. But when he asked about my sexual fantasies, I took a potentially lethal overdose. My marriage fell apart. Although I was still in individual and group therapy in 1974, Bill began a social entanglement with me that ended only when he married his third wife and moved away in 1979. Without him I grew stronger, divorced, retrained as a broadcast journalist and found a loving partner.

Then, in 1989, I discovered a photo of Bill and me dancing together. And diaries from 1977 and 1978.

August 29, 1977
... visited Bill and [his second wife]. Invited to drink wine and smoke marijuana [I was still taking his prescribed drugs]. Bill then invited me

to dinner alone with him. ... During a conversation said he'd like to "play mind games" and "do poppers and acid" with me.

Other entries described floating naked in his isolation tank, harvesting marijuana according to his instructions, being invited to a midnight ceremony for his dead mother, sharing sexual fantasies of whips, leather boots and sexy underwear over late-night drinks, setting up a sexual threesome at his request.

The relationship, mimicking incest, made me decide to formally complain. Unfortunately, I sent the letter to the wrong doctors' association. They forwarded it to Bill, who responded to me:

> I have always hold you in high asteem [sic]. ... In all our therapy hours (nearly 200) and our continuing friendship I have always worked toward your eventual happiness and well-being.

Claiming not to remember the party depicted in the photo, he wrote, "I drank too much (an error in judgement). Love, Bill."

I readdressed my letter to the College of Physicians and Surgeons of Ontario (CPSO). Although I knew nothing about it, a new task force had just formed to examine how cases of physician-patient abuse were handled. Mine was the task force's first complaint.

The CPSO's chief investigator flew out to coastal BC, where I now lived, to question me. He took my signed statement along with the cards and gifts Bill gave me, my diaries and the photograph from the "forgotten" party where we got drunk and stoned together and he danced so close I could feel his erection before he slipped his hand under me as we sat on the couch.

"There'll be a long inquiry into your allegations," the investigator said, "but we've got enough to nail him."

On May 2, 1991, he filed a report with a memo to his boss:

> Although there is still follow-up work to do, it is time to notify the doctor of Ms. Ashby-Rolls's exact complaint, and get his response to the issues presented.

Bill did respond, categorically denying my allegations—with one exception:

> I may have attended a social function hosted by a group member at which Ms. Ashby-Rolls was present. ... If marijuana was used, I was not aware of it. ... My behaviour towards her has always been professional. ...

A year later, CPSO's Complaints Committee sent my case for hearing under the Health Disciplines Act. I had to wait three more years.

Meanwhile, CPSO sought a medical opinion "regarding the standard of psychiatric care provided" by Bill, and a review of "the impact of sexualizing the relationship on Ms. Ashby-Rolls's mental state." Psychiatrist Dr. Diane Watson did the assessment. In her report, she validated the damage Bill caused me, noting my "intense reaction to events which occurred almost twenty years ago. ... There is no reason to doubt the authenticity of Ms. Ashby-Rolls's recall or legitimacy of her interpretation of events." She described the negative, destructive effects of doctors who sexually exploit their patients.

I flew to Toronto in January 1995 with a friend. The lawyer acting on behalf of CPSO, Michelle Fuerst, said Bill would plead guilty to everything but sexual impropriety. I wanted my day in court.

Bill appeared smaller than I remembered—something to do with the power I'd given him. Members of the public and news media were present as he stood before a disciplinary panel made up of three physicians and two government-appointed laypeople. Outlining the case, Ms. Fuerst focused on boundary violations. Bill's lawyer, Niels Ortved, said the heart of the matter was "the charge of sexual impropriety." A technical argument ensued about whether my diaries should be entered as evidence. The panel deemed them of no interest. Fuerst used portions from them as if from "a hypothetical case."

That evening, a news anchor reported, "Allegations of kinky sex, illicit drugs and cult involvement were made at the first day of a disciplinary hearing today, against the psychiatrist-in-chief at the Scarborough General Hospital. The complainant, Trysh Ashby-Rolls, testified that Doctor William Henry Longdon had asked her to arrange a sexual triangle involving her, the doctor and another woman. According to the testimony, Dr. Longdon is alleged to have said that he and Ashby-Rolls would kidnap the woman if necessary, chain her up and force her to comply. The hearing is expected to last a week."

On the stand, I broke years of silence. Asked why I had waited so long to complain, I said, "I felt far too fragile. ... I kept the photo till I was strong enough." I never forgot what happened after confronting Jumbo.

Ortved's strategy was to confuse me. Fuerst said he was framing his questions to say I was lying and threatened to bring my diaries into court. But when he suggested, "sexual toys are something with which you have lots of familiarity," she banged on the table.

"Objection. This witness's other experiences are not relevant," she yelled, quoting from the 1992 Supreme Court of Canada's rape shield law ruling that restricts a defence lawyer's ability to question alleged victims of sexual assault about their past sexual history.

Shame enveloped me when Ortved asked how Bill got his hand under my skirt to fondle my genitals. As if a hand gripped my throat to stop me speaking, a voice inside said, "You colluded in your own seduction." After all, it was Bill who tried to make me responsible for being raped in Spain, so how could I admit to hitching up my own skirt? Or that I wore no panties underneath?

When expert witness, Dr. Nancy Price-Munn, took the stand Ortved baited her mercilessly, twice addressing her as *Miss* Price-Munn. "I find it amusing," she said, "that you are incapable of addressing me, a woman, by my correct title, Doctor."

She pointed out the many occasions where Bill lost the opportunity "to interpret and explore [which is] the heart of therapy." Later, causing suppressed laughter, she said, "There is no such thing as a benign or philanthropic penis."

Nobody cracked even a smile when she described how vulnerable I was to physician-patient victimization. "Three psychiatrists knew Ms. Ashby-Rolls had been sexually abused. She was a sitting duck."

Next, Bill took the stand. Ortved urged him to speak up. Indeed, made him practise until everyone heard his description of me when we met in 1972. He said he agreed with Jumbo's diagnosis: autistic and schizophrenic.

"Darling, I'd call you many things, but never autistic," my friend whispered.

"I think he means artistic," I whispered back. Bill flushed scarlet.

He stumbled and stuttered over his words, couldn't read his own notes when asked to quote from them. One note, which he managed to decipher, shocked me. Apparently, he'd made me sit in a chair in his office repeating, "I love to masturbate." Clearly, it distressed me deeply; the incident remains a blank. His notes, mostly about sex, merited only a brief mention of my suicide attempt as a "self-poisoning episode." Of his marijuana use he said, "I smoke dope occasionally for recreational purposes."

"Did you have an improper social relationship with Ms. Ashby-Rolls?"

"Yep."

He denied being sexual with me, or having feelings about me.

"Did you find Ms. Ashby-Rolls attractive?"

He didn't answer.

"In your note about session number one, December 11, 1972, you wrote, 'Ms. Ashby-Rolls is beautiful, a classic beauty.' Did you find Ms. Ashby-Rolls attractive?"

He still didn't answer, then burst out, "I found Ms. Ashby-Rolls attractive. I find Ms. Ashby-Rolls attractive. Anyone would find Ms. Ashby-Rolls attractive."

Instinctively, I crossed my legs and folded my arms across my breasts. In front of a roomful of onlookers his words reduced me to an object, naked and exposed. Like in therapy with him all those years ago.

Another female patient from the therapy group identified Bill and me in the photo. Questioned about the party, she contended that nothing untoward happened. However, during cross-examination, she revealed that wine and liqueurs were consumed and everyone, except her, smoked marijuana—including Bill.

After the closing arguments it took the disciplinary panel less than an hour to return its verdict: Guilty to the majority of charges against him, including failing to maintain a standard of practice, professional incompetence, disgraceful, dishonourable conduct unbecoming a physician. Not guilty of sexual impropriety. Under the influence of marijuana and too much alcohol I'd got muddled about the sexual fondling.

I felt defeated, as though I'd been found guilty. I wanted to walk away knowing I'd done all I could to right a wrong, not go home disempowered. I asked to make a statement before the penalty phase.

My voice was strong as I began: "Ladies and gentlemen, the word discipline comes from the Latin *disciplinare*, meaning to learn."

I outlined into a pin-dropping silence what I'd learned over the past week about humiliation, communication, the subjective nature of reality, the power of diagnostic labels, definition of words, about memory, truth telling, truth being a various thing; the fancy footwork of lawyers; taking responsibility, being accountable; about integrity and courage. I spoke about returning to therapy in 1988, how I'd coped between ending therapy with Bill and starting over again.

People sniffed, blew their noses, blinked back tears. I described how three counsellors—one a man—had discussed with me at the first session their boundaries, rights and responsibilities and the nature of the therapeutic relationship. I talked about my career, how I'd trained doctors and spoken at international conferences about working with survivors of child sexual abuse, and I talked about writing.

Without wiping away the tears streaming down his face, Bill gazed at me. I understood then what I'd wanted from him all those years ago: to be heard and respected.

Bill's licence was suspended for six months, with conditions. He was required to give a series of seminars to his staff on boundary violations and he was to tell new patients the boundaries and expectations of the therapy contract. He waived his right to appeal.

A strong message was sent to doctors that behaviour like Bill's, even if it happened decades ago, would not be tolerated. I won a tremendous, precedent-setting victory.

Ruth Johnston

A STORY WITHOUT THE WORD "NO" SPOKEN ALOUD

He was possessed by love and imagined
he had no options: my body burned
in his heart like an answer. He gave me
glow. He gave me all the significance
of a saint or a new life. He parted my legs,
tore into me like holy water
he hoped to drown in,
and I sank into silence
like a trinket lost in the sea.

Editor's Note: The first line is heavily inspired by a line in By Grand Central Station
I Sat Down and Wept *by Elizabeth Smart*

Sara Graefe

FIERCE

She always appears during those long car rides, sort of slips out from under my skin as mile after mile of cattle field whizzes by, a snow-covered blur. He's taking us further and further from our day selves in the city—the brown brick high school where he's the gentle, caring teacher everyone likes and I'm his student, the girl on the honour roll. He likes me because of my talent. My sweet smile. Or so he says.

There are rules to this game. This car ride the inevitable ritual. We always start with something safe: small talk about school, Cat Stevens singing "Peace Train" on the radio. But it's always a different road, one I've never seen before, so I wouldn't have a clue how to get back if I tried. You'd think I'd have learned to pay attention by now, trace a map in my head so I'd know where the hell I was, where he's taking me. Hansel and Gretel, except I always forget the bread crumbs. *Stupid fairy tale*. I'm sixteen, too old for that kind of thing anyway. Maybe it's that windy feeling I get in my head when we're well past the city limits, tumbledown barns and rickety fences, me and him alone in his Honda, driving.

She's always there when the wind stops. He sneaks a glance at me across the seat. It's as though he knows she's there now too. It's part of the game. But he has to pretend not to see her. Not just yet.

By now he's different, too. I'd rather not know but she sees, she tells me. That's why she has to be there. Because he's different, too.

He meets my eyes. "If you knew what I was really like, you'd hate me."

"No, I won't," I lie. The scripted answer. Do I even say it out loud? But I feel her inside, fighting every word. But she doesn't say anything. Not just yet.

"What would I do without you?" He reaches across the vinyl seat and grabs my hand.

Once I would've been flattered. The way my heart used to tingle when he'd keep me after class and tell me I was beautiful. But now I only feel his sweaty grip, the way he's holding on and not letting go, my hand limp and fragile but he keeps squeezing like his life depended on it.

He's staring deep into my eyes now. Penetrating blue. But I can't hold his stare, it's too much. I look quickly away, out the passenger window, silently willing him to get his eyes back on the road. *Not now, not in the car, we're going to crash...*

On and on he drives. It's quiet now. The radio has crackled out of range. The silence is unnerving, but he likes it.

"Isn't it amazing when two people are so connected that they don't even need words anymore?" he observes.

"Yes," I say quietly, not knowing how else to respond. It's true and yet it's not; he's twisted it around somehow. I don't really want to know where he's going with this but I feel her inside again, resigning now, giving over. And as she goes, she sweeps me away with her, like undertow. This is how it always happens.

He pulls over at a gas station. Two rusty Esso pumps and a store in an old house. "Fred's 24-hour Groceteria," the sign proclaims. "Open Under New Management." I laugh inside in spite of myself. I don't know if it's the drive or what, but by this time the world seems tilted on its side. Like the new management who've obviously tried to fix up the store with brand new siding, but have got it wrong somehow. The aluminum too plastic, the grey too bright. Anyone can tell how ugly and rundown it still is, underneath it all.

I follow him inside and linger by the teen magazines, skimming "How to French Kiss" while he buys some pop. Diet Coke, two cans, one for me and one for him.

"My daily fix," he laughs, guiltily. "My wife's been trying to get me off the sweets." He's a heavy man alright. His stomach's always protruding over his belt. "But hell," he adds, "it's my only vice. At least it's diet."

I feel her cringe, inside. "Yeah," I shrug, not knowing what else to say. "At least it's diet." But as I sip my drink in the parking lot, the liquid burns my throat. I choke and gag and spit it out, the brown fluid melting the snow, the aftertaste like mothballs. I check over my shoulder, hoping he hasn't noticed.

But he's busy, filling the car with gas. He whistles along to some tune I don't know, rattling the keys in his pocket. I think for a moment about running away but I am trapped in the game now. The gas pump rumbles, labouring away, and I kick the frozen gravel with my sneakers. I watch the stones fly in perfect arcs and try not to think about what she knows. The inevitability of this ritual.

She knows that in the middle of the night there's no going back.

They're the rules of the game but in the middle of the night I can never play anymore, it hurts too much. I slip away and leave her to it. It's always her mouth, he thinks I'll stay a virgin that way, gagging, choking, her jaw locked open and she's *afraid like me,* afraid that the force will smother her. His head down her throat and she's fighting now, fighting and he doesn't even care because he's not really there, he's in some dark place where even she can't reach. Even though she sees. Even though she knows. But it's late and she wants to go home now, she wants my soft bed, she wants somewhere safe.

Stop! Help! No!

I don't really hear her. I pretend to be asleep. Close my eyes tight and keep the ugliness out.

In the morning, he sees only me. This is how he fools himself. "You're such an angel," he says, his whole body aglow, reaching down to stroke my hair as I sit there in his old farmhouse kitchen. He hums as he makes me breakfast: blueberry waffles dripping with syrup. He doesn't even notice that she's still there, hovering by the stove, watching his every move. Senses on hyper-alert.

I catch glimpses of her, lingering in my peripheral vision. She's fading, though, losing her strength. She can no longer speak, her jaw aches too much. But she is fierce. Her presence makes me uneasy.

He always takes the long way back to school to extend the ritual as much as possible. I wouldn't notice if he didn't point it out, it'd just be another road I don't know, more snow and more endless fields.

"If only it could always be like this," he says, eyes glistening, lamenting the return to our day selves. He looks like he might start to cry. I quickly look away. He expects me to agree, of course, but this time I have nothing to say. I, too, have tired of the game. It's as though she's stuck in my throat now. I cough, involuntarily. And once I start, I can't seem to stop.

He brushes my cheek. "Are you OK?"

I swallow her down and nod, try to avoid his probing stare. Keep my eyes straight ahead, drink in the rays of sun reflecting off the snow.

As we near the school, all that's left now is her whisper. Or is that the wind whistling through my head again? I wish I could just blow away with her, but he holds on to me as long as possible. As we pull into the school parking lot, I am flooded with relief—it's finally over. But no, he eases the Honda into his usual spot, cuts the ignition. "Let's not go in just yet."

I sit with him in silence. An eternity. Yearning to escape, run through the big glass doors into the school. Lose him in the rows of bright yellow lockers, the buzz of voices and girlish giggles in the halls. Return to myself, the girl on the honour roll.

Instead, he grabs me, pulling me tight into his chest. Holds me so close that I can hear his heart beating, fast. He's desperate now, I can feel it in the way he envelops me. He doesn't want to let me go because then the game will be over.

At least for now.

Out of the corner of my eye, I become aware of somebody watching. My music teacher, Mr. Pattison, walking by in the parking lot. I freeze, caught with him in that sick embrace. My mind starts racing. I wonder how much Mr. P. saw. What he thinks. Whether he'll tell.

Who he sees. Me or her?

David Fraser

LITTLE STARS

Out of the moonlight
princesses primp,
preen and perch
upon pedestals.
Stars dazzle
in their hair.
In pink dresses and
glitter shoes,
they masquerade
before their parents'
daring dreams.
But in the spectrum
of the lights above
their eyes betray
a feather lost
from an angel's wing.
Each heart is
beating for a random
exit door,
where grandma, time-lapse
cuts
the star apple
with a kitchen knife
and the two of them have tea.

Yasuko Thanh

HOOKED

I sat on an overturned milk crate in the sunshine the summer I was seventeen. Champagne, my friend, cursed the circle jerks, the men who drove around the block at Richards and Seymour, looked at the hookers but never stopped to take us out.

She bent over, rubbed her toes through the leather of her stilettos. I was barefoot. I sucked on a Dole strawberry juice bar and monitored my tan through my sunglasses. My six-inch heels lay in the shadow of the Korner Kitchen coffee shop, flung aside. I slathered my legs with baby oil.

"My man's going to kill me," she said. "I need to make at least four."

I already had three hundred dollars in my bra; the roll of bills made my breasts itchy.

Champagne worked double-shifts, six days a week. In contrast, I worked three-hour days, four days a week.

I'd never had a *really* bad date. Champagne had been kidnapped by people who had bound her with rope and held her for two days in a garage; they forced her to eat dog food. A man with a station wagon and a child's car seat in the back had cracked Shelley's head open with a crowbar in the alley behind General Paints. She had returned to work with seventy-two stitches on her head that she had tried to hide under a French twist, and a cast on her arm from blocking blows.

My pimp had not been around, maybe dancing at the Cotton Club, when these things happened. It didn't matter, because I was in control. I was careful, which counted for more than luck, and I was sure it would never happen to me.

I wore silk and ate lobster. I wasn't a victim.

One day I'm hanging by my neck from the living-room wall in our suite at the Robsonstrasse Hotel and I don't want to believe it.

I was wearing a sweater given to me by a trick. I don't like the colour beige, but I was fond of Holt Renfrew and because it was an expensive store, I liked the label, sewn into the collar of the garment. I was smoking a cigarette and as he hung me up from my neck, the cigarette burned uselessly there, in my hand, the smoke spiralling. I never once thought to butt it out in his eye. Somehow the cherry singed my cashmere sweater but it wouldn't be until the next day that I'd notice the hole in the sleeve and sit down in a brown armchair with worn upholstery—the varnish, like all the furniture in the West End room, dull with age and use—to stitch the edges of it back together with the wrong coloured thread.

I would remain with him another seven years and this neck-hanging would be simply the first. Over the span of our relationship, I always forgave him because:

He'd had a rough childhood.

He always hit me with an open hand, never with a closed fist.

He'd had six siblings, all different fathers.

I was an awful cook.

He'd been thrown into adult jail for two years less a day as a teenager.

I kept terrible house.

He'd been beaten for being half-Cree, half-Jamaican in a white neighbourhood.

I was sassy.

I had been an honour roll student. The *Times Colonist* had written an article about my academic, athletic and civic achievements. A skinny column featuring a grainy picture that I hated, my skinny face, acne and poodle perm. My parents had saved the clipping and, before gluing it into the pages of a family scrapbook, had sent photocopies to aunts and uncles in Germany and France and California. In one year, I went from training bras and knee socks to latex corsets and half-and-halfs for two hundred dollars.

The first time he beat me, I hadn't been afraid, but shocked. I'd felt surprised that people really did this kind of thing to each other.

I told the friends who didn't understand why I stayed, "It's easy to love if you only look at what's loveable." Did I really say those words?

Ten years later, they sometimes still feel true.

The library is full of self-help books on forgiveness: *The Art of Forgiveness, From Anger to Intimacy, How Forgiveness Can Transform Your Marriage*. I could quote from them by heart. They said I didn't have to forgive and forget, I just had to let go of the resentment around which my life had begun to revolve.

Let go? I couldn't even leave the house. But him, I loved.

We met when I was sixteen and he was twenty-seven. I translated apartment leases or stereo rental agreements for him because he couldn't read well. My mother, who had no idea, thought he was charming and laughed at his jokes.

He said we'd always be together, "Unless I kill you and baby, believe me,

I would do time for killing you." Mostly, I thought this was romantic.

Now I am older than he was when we split up, a mother of two. My partner knows all about me and loves me anyway.

I was homeless at fifteen.

Raped by a man who felt he hadn't got his one hundred dollars worth.

Dragged by my hair from a moving car by someone unhappy with my blow job.

Beaten on the street by a stranger with an umbrella who had gone off his medication.

The list could go on. We live in a three-bedroom townhouse with colourful walls. I have Chalkware in the shape of apples and sparrows in my kitchen. We have a collection of LPs twelve-feet long. We have a TV from the '50s. It doesn't work, so we're thinking of turning it into a fish tank. We have the how-to book.

Crazy, skid row or in jail, is where I thought we'd all end-up. My ex? He got married. He works in a car-parts store in eastern Canada.

All the money I earned is gone.

Only one pimp I knew stacked his money. He kept it in a briefcase under his bed—over half a million, I heard. More than that amount passed through my hands on its way to my pimp's hands and then into his pockets. I barely felt it: paper's light, doesn't feel like much in the palm. I'm still trying to measure its true weight. What did it all mean? I wonder if that pimp with the briefcase ever got to spend his cash. I wonder if he got his money's worth.

David Fraser

ONE LADY LOST

Atlantis, Reno
From this lost place of paradise
she rises from the lush carpet
seafoam from the wave,
her earth a jaded, consumptive
shore of gluttony.
She hears the siren's call,
deposited from the shuttle bus,
the ferry to this neon underworld
of flashing lights;
dressed out of season and indoors,
fur hat, earflaps, flightless wings,
heavy boots, red wool, arms,
a too-long sweater scuffed,
purse gaping wide, cradled.
She is so out of step with the click of poker chips,
the jingle of the coins
streaming from the slots,
the buffet stuffing bellies
dribbling mouths, bloating in
this seedy paradise of excess pain.
She wanders up and down the aisles,
her winter gear as shocking as
the bruises on her face,
the lesions locked within her heart.

Ruth Carrier

FIREBALL

I was brought up in the Depression of 1930 amid physical and sexual beatings from my father. I was fifth of eleven kids, and the older ones had already left an unhappy home before I did at age twenty-one.

I had little education, as my father didn't think it necessary. I was "only good for factory work" so I only went up to Grade Eight. Yes, factory work, which eventually led to work in a small office. But I kept my nose to the grindstone and gradually got slightly better jobs.

In my mid-thirties I started having a slight affair with a fellow from our company who worked in BC. I met him at the office in Toronto. It was pleasant for some time—dancing, dinner, pleasant sex—until we went to the movies one evening and saw *The Exorcist*. Gosh, a film had never disgusted me and frightened me as much as this one.

When we got back to my apartment, my "friend" immediately became amorous. I wasn't moved; I was still thinking of the film. I wanted the guy to leave but he kept pressing on me, took off his jacket. Please, just one kiss and he'd leave. The one kiss was so aggressive I gave a low scream in my throat while he pressed himself on me. I'd rescued a kitten some five years before, and I suddenly heard a loud growl. A growl? I thought. Where on earth would the growl come from?

Then my "friend" became more aggressive, I let out a louder, though still muffled scream. He was going to rape me! A split second later, this guy let out a horrid, loud scream, immediately let go of me, turned, grabbed his coat, apologized and fled. My cat had jumped on his back and dug her claws into his back and probably used her teeth as well.

This all took just seconds. I was stunned. I watched this guy make a hasty retreat then looked down at my beloved pet, a grey short-haired alley cat. She was rubbing herself back and forth against my leg, purring very loudly, and her short, smooth fur was standing on end so much that she looked for all the world like a fat Persian!

I've never forgotten that. Yes, pets can and do save their owners. Fireball was a great cat and loveable little friend.

Michelle Demers

LIFE IN JAIL

Interview by Emma Cochrane

How long were you in jail for?

January 27 to July 27, 1989. I got a nine-month sentence. I did six months, three months good behaviour—you do two-thirds of your time, right? Did it in Oakalla. Oakalla was ripped down in 1994.

I built the dog program when I was in jail. They started this dog program where they brought in four dogs from the SPCA and you trained 'em. They got four inmates and they would have them totally involved with these four dogs. They had to adopt them in jail, sort of, and they had to train them, and they would go into their cell with them. They were either badly beaten or heavily abused animals. They had a lady, two ladies, come in, and CBC, the news, came in too. It was the first tryout for this; they were doing it for the girls to try and they knew I was a carpenter so they asked me if I could go in and build all these obstacles and build them a kennel for the dogs to stay in at night 'cause they could only have the inmates in their cells till a certain time, then they all had to take them back to their kennels. So, I had to build a kennel and all these obstacles for them. And it was kinda cool.

They've adopted this dog program all over Canada now. I think we were the initial people that tried it and they put big publicity on it. It was rehab the dogs and rehab the girls—especially with women that had trouble, or had been abused themselves. You know, they needed something to love and to love them back unconditionally.

It was the first program of its kind in Canada and they wanted to see if it would work out and help the inmates and the dogs. And, of course it did help the inmates and the dogs. And it just kept rolling.

That was kinda cool building that; made my time go a little easier. There wasn't much aside from building that and getting laid—that's all there is to do in jail, let me tell ya. I'm serious. There's a lot of women in there.

How many women are in a tier and how many tiers in the prison?

In Oakalla, there were six tiers. You'd go in the one unit when you came in and they'd decide where you should go from there. Unit seven is the big hardcore tier. I think there's sixty girls on that unit. There's two showers, one at each end, and it's one whole floor but it's cut into two tiers, with eight locks and big doors. Lotsa concrete, lotsa iron metal, bars and stuff. It was the old jail. Women only. Then there was another tier that was called unit eight and then there's unit six, where you come in on. There's unit three. They sorta break it up so that if somebody like you came in—you're pretty small and petite and feminine—they'd stick you in three probably. You know, a nice, mellow unit, with the little old ladies. Blue-collar-crime ladies.

There was one lady in there that went into some bar and got drunk and said, "I wanna hire somebody to kill my husband," and there was an undercover in the crowd and he came up to her. She was doing time and she was in her sixties. Some of those things are sad; she just said she was tired of him beating on her and that now that all the kids had grown up and gone away, she was gonna kill him. She'd had enough.

Ninety percent of the women that are in there are in jail for killing their spouses. And they got the most bizarre stories: "He fell on the knife eleven times." I had to laugh at that one [laughs]. That was one of my roommates. I said, "Do you think you're gonna get away with it?" "Oh, yeah, yeah."

People have the wildest stories, but a lot of women are in there for killing their man. Or for killing the girl that was with their man. It can get pretty violent, eh? But, most of them in there have been violated. They've been raped, they've been beaten and there's a lot of repeaters. There's the lifer crowd—the people that are doing ten years or more, or over five years, or four, or whatever. Manslaughter is a minimum of four; self-defence is a minimum of two years less a day. You got the hard timers that are in there and then you got the repeaters.

The repeaters are all the hookers downtown. They get grabbed all the time; they like to get grabbed; they like to come in and repeat. They get called repeaters, you don't call them hookers in jail. They like to repeat 'cause they get medical, dental all free, free meals, free cot. You know, they can relax, they don't have to worry about pimps and johns and that bullshit, and they're usually all heroin addicts. You get a lot of heroin in that jail. There's hardly any cocaine that goes in there. It's all heroin. Can't smoke pot in there, it stinks, so you know, you do what you do.

They're just in and out but like fucking gum to your shoe. Two weeks to a month. Can't get rid of them. Just keep comin' in about every three weeks. And you say, "Weren't you just in here?" "Yeah, I just left." Okay, fine.

Then there's people that are in there for drugs, armed robberies, stuff like that. They're pretty fucked-up people, too. Everybody that goes in there is pretty fucked-up people.

I didn't think I was that fucked-up, I just liked making money. I liked having a big pocket full of it; nice cars, nice trucks, you know. I worked hard in life too, right? Built houses and commercial buildings and stuff, a lot of stuff. I didn't think after twenty-two years that I'd get caught. But somebody ratted me out and that was it.

And there were nine charges or something against me. But, you know, you pay the lawyer the big bucks and he's supposed to get you off, no problem. I got busted, went to jail, had to pay all this stuff—fifteen grand immediately—and waited eleven months for the trial. The lawyer said, "It's not a problem. Don't worry about it, I got you covered." He never said anything to me the whole eleven months. Twenty minutes in the courtroom he says, "They're making an example of you," because of course the informant called me "Michelle the dyke." So, right then and there I was called "Michelle the dyke" about four or five times.

So I was kinda pissed when I got in Oakalla. When I walked into jail, I was lookin' for a fight. I walked up and down the tiers just looking. I stayed in the one unit—you usually only go in there for three to six days and then they decide where you should go, what tier. Well, they couldn't decide. They were too afraid to talk to me, even come near me. So about six weeks later, I'm still walking up and down. And they say to me "Well, fuck, we know you're looking for a fight." And I would walk up and down and say, "Hey, make my fucking day, I wanna kill something, come on."

And you get these big fucking dykes and they're in there for life and they're fucking pumping weights and they'd take a girl like you, just this tiny little girl, who's just in there for like two weeks because of an impaired or something stupid, or for getting caught with a couple of joints or something. Well, fuck, this is not the environment to send her to. They'd send people like you in there and then these big fucking ugly dykes would say, "You're mine. You like that [gestures to her groin], you get me coffee. You clean my cell. You do whatever I tell you to do; you're my girl. Or you'll get fucking shit-kicked every day until you tell me that you want to be with me."

Of course, I don't like that kind of situation, so this perks up my interest for a fight. So I say, "Hey, she doesn't wanna fucking be with you, she doesn't know you from a hole in the ground. If that's how you gotta be with women, you got a fucking problem. Now you're dealing with me. She ain't with you, she's with me. Fuck you. Come on."

She backs off right away, and I think, Oh, fuck, 'cause nobody would fight me. Everyone'd say the same thing, "We wanna be your friend," and I'd say, "I don't want no fucking friends in here. I wanna kill someone." Nobody would fight me.

Even the guards came up to me and said, "Michelle, everyone's afraid of you, including the guards. Everybody's afraid of you; we don't know where to put you. We're afraid you're going to kill somebody."

Is there a lot of sexual violence?

No, no, everybody's pretty passive. But any woman that goes in there—I don't care what woman you are—things happen. You can say, "Yeah, I'm straighter than straight," but what happens in jail, usually stays in jail. Especially for a lot of women that are married or whatever, they get out and they go back to their lives with husbands or boyfriends and what happened in jail, stays in jail. Everybody hooks up. Cell mates. Guards are doing guards, guards are doing inmates. I was doing guards, I was doing inmates, I was doing them all. It's a fucking fuck fest in there.

I mean everybody's so fucked on heroin, it's ridiculous. They're getting it in there quite a bit, lots of it, and everybody gets pretty mellow on that shit. You know, lovey and mellow and it's a good way to spend your time in there. Good shit to do when you're bored and you got nothing better to do.

What kind of group did you fit into?

I didn't. I had my own group: me. But everyone wanted to be like me, or everyone wanted to hang out with me or be my friend because I was this person that walked up and down the tiers looking for a fight and nobody'd fight me.

There wasn't too much mixing, know what I mean? There was a lot of fighting that went on, territorial things: you can't have that, you can have this, this sort of deal; that's my girl, no that's my girl. "I saw her first"-type action.

Certain tiers got certain things, more than anybody else. Like these guys here got hot dogs, and we didn't. You get kind of aggressive and possessive over the simplest, stupidest things like food and bread, you know. It's fucking crazy. You got nothing else to fight about.

And there were groups where everyone's slamming their cups on the table and gashing their arms open with the shards. You know, you got twelve of them doing it and its like, let's see what the guards can do. Let's fuck up the guards tonight. Let's see how many ambulances they can get to Oakalla.

Everybody's into getting shit started, big time. And then there's blood flying, guards grabbing girls, glass flying everywhere. It's like a big escape thing too, because now girls can get a night out in a hospital. So they gotta call the guards to come in to the hospital.

As soon as that kinda of shit goes down, everybody goes on lockdown. *Beep beep beep beep.* Guards are flying everywhere—you gotta lock down now. You gotta be in your cell and you gotta be on lockdown. So they got two guards locking down every tier. They grab you, they handcuff you, they fucking ankle cuff you, grab you by the fucking chain, drag you down on the belly, head first into the digger. It's just a cell and a toilet and a sink. That's it. Nothing else. No pillows, no blankets, no mattress.

What's the relationship between the guards and the inmates?

The guards all wanted to be friends with all the inmates. That's the way they wanted it. Some of the inmates were pretty mean sons of bitches because they're in there for murder and stuff. There's a lot of tension there. You don't know what you're walking into the next day and what could've transpired the night before or during the night. You ask, "What happened last night?"

"Oh, everyone tried to commit suicide with a bunch of fucking coffee cups, so we're taking all the coffee cups away." So then we're all walking around with fucking plastic cups; its degrading as all hell. So, now you got some people real pissed off.

There's lots of fights, just lots of fights. Someone tried to stab me with a fork over a plate of meat. We get a plate of meat, a plate of potatoes on the table, and this very large Indian woman, she came out of her cell only at meal times, she'd come out and take the plate of meat. At breakfast we'd have a plate of sausage or bacon and a plate of eggs, and then one with toast. And every morning, she'd grab the plate of meat and dump it in her bag. And I'd think, fuck, I didn't get no bacon. The next meal, it'd be something else. It was getting out of control, so, fuck it, she's not taking any more meat.

So I sat beside her and as soon as the guard put down the plate and I went to grab it, this woman tried to stab me in the arm. Well, I took her fork away from her, threw it on the ground and that's it. She threw her arm around me and tried to get me by the throat and kill me. I just let down the plate, pushed it over on the table and said, "Here you go, you guys, everyone gets meat tonight," and I started wailing on this girl.

By then, the guards are all up on and around us, trying to get over the table and get us apart. I was in the digger for a couple days on that one too. But that's okay. I fought my point. And after that they served us individual portions. No more big plates on the table so we all got something of everything.

You know, now that I'm older I sometimes think, how did I survive all that? I think it was just the mindset, I think. Just knowing that I'm a tough son of a bitch and I'm gonna take you out. To me, it's life or death. It's me or you. As far as I'm concerned, it was you. It's gonna take a lot to put me down. And I know that: I'm a tough, mean son of a bitch.

Brittany Luby

AN INTRODUCTION TO YOUTH

I would like to introduce you to a little girl:

She has dirty-blond hair and green eyes. She speaks quickly and sleeps in a single bed. She has named her favourite stuffed toys Lucky and King. Her mother is pretty. Her father is slim. For a child, she's "quite a looker." She never kept her baby fat and has to wear an undershirt, long sleeves and a sweater to keep warm. She is too thin and wears mittens in the house. She plays with an older lady who has a fort in the bush. They play special games. Sometimes she is a kitten sucking on teats. Sometimes she is a mommy making babies. Sometimes she is sad, but never says so. When she cries the woman sings *lullay lullay*. Four other girls play too. They are her age and "pritt-y." These girls dance like the twelve dancing princesses. It helps them to keep warm when their clothes are off. The girl hopes that her mother will come to huff and to puff and to blow the fort down. But Mommy never does.

The place is hidden and the tale too unlikely to be true.

Leah Fowler

LEARNING TO LIE

Is it necessary for me to write obliquely
about the situation? Is that what
you would have me do?
—Adrienne Rich, "Dark Fields of the Republic"

Chalk poised on blackboard, midway in a sentence about plot structure, I glimpse a Grade Ten girl as she tries to slip quietly into my English classroom after the bell has gone. We have a late policy in our school, so I stop her before she gets through the door.

"Where were you?" I demand, elbows jutting akimbo.

Then I notice the twig and dried leaf in her left running shoe. I notice her eyes. The image of my five-year-old self comes back to me.

~

"Where were you?" my mother demands, way back then. Her elbows jut akimbo.

I stand an arm's length from her, notice the dark purple teardrops in my new paisley cotton dress and smooth them twice with both hands, from the waist to below my knees.

And wait.

"Well?"

I notice a piece of twig with one dried, dark brown leaf, wedged in the tiny buckle of my new black patent leather shoes. I slide that shoe behind the other so she can't see it. I clear my throat, look at her shoes bigger and wider than mine. Red with tall spiked heels. I wonder how she walks in them without falling. I guess she may even buy a pair for me, before I am ready.

It helps to imagine her catching a heel in one of the grates in the sidewalk on Main Street beside the new Eaton's store where she got my dress. In my mind she falls, hits her head and bleeds to match her shoes. Still in my imagination, I calmly call for an ambulance, collect her purse and gloves, ride with them, wait in the emergency waiting room for news of her demise.

"I'm only going to ask you once more. Where were you?"

I know she will ask more than once and I stop myself from sighing. For a moment I consider telling her, but see something in the pressure in the line between her lips, see that dangerous darkness behind the narrowed pale blue eyes. Possible answers begin to type themselves across the back of my vision, like telegrams of newspaper headlines:

"Local child playing with dog called Shadow in garden"

"Little girl looking at books on front porch"

"Small child upstairs visiting grandmother"

"Girl and man playing hide and seek in yard"

No, not that one: too close. The mind-telegrams begin to come in blank, out of ink. I worry about being questioned about the twig stuck in my shoe, so I tip the other heel up and press it to better hide the leaf and twig. Later, when she isn't looking, I will clean my shoes, and flush the twig and leaf down the toilet.

"How many times have I told you never to go out of the yard? I called and called you but no little girl appeared. So where WERE you?"

The back porch door squeaks open, then slams shut.

We both glance upstairs. It might be my father, so now two questioners. They will talk between themselves about what should be done with me. But it's not my father; it's "him." I hear him talking in the kitchen, above us.

I know I must never tell.

"If you can't answer me, maybe you'll go to bed without any supper. Think about being bad. Good little girls answer their mothers nicely. Jesus doesn't like bad little girls. Well?"

No, not well. I think about Jesus's picture on our church sanctuary wall behind where the preacher talks—Jesus's face is looking skyward, with soft brown beard, long flowing hair, brown robe. The colours in my aunt's paint box appear in my mind: sepia, ochre, burnt sienna, burnt umber. I am pretty sure the Jesus picture doesn't have anything to do with me.

But what if my mother is right? What if the man in the picture doesn't like me and will punish me for being bad? I close my left fist more tightly around the peppermint, not wanting to be asked about that either. I bend over, pull up my white knee socks and hide the peppermint inside the elastic behind my left knee.

"Answer me. What were you doing when I called you?"

I wonder how long we will stand here together before she sends me to my bed in the corner of the kitchen to turn my face to the wall. I can lift the little brass door on the water meter there and see the numbers tick by. I wonder how they measure water. Could you trick the meter by running the water very fast? Would you have to run it really slowly so the little mechanism they put inside wouldn't notice much.

Since I can't see the seams at the back of my mother's nylons, I am pretty sure she can't see the peppermint lump in the back of my sock. I will wait until she is busy later, carefully timing when I put my panties into the laundry. I think about flushing them, like the leaf and twig, but am afraid they will not go down. It would be worse if my father uses the big, red plunger and they came floating to the surface again. I don't think I can get away with throwing them out.

I wait, hands clasped together in front of my dress.

I wish I were wearing my navy blue jodhpurs. I don't like how dresses make me feel.

"If you can't learn to tell the truth, they won't take you in kindergarten next year. You know you want to go there like Margaret, to colour and read books and learn your numbers. Where were you? I want you to TELL ME RIGHT NOW!"

Already I know my letters and numbers. I can read a little; they don't know that yet either. Instead I concentrate on remembering that her voice doesn't always sound like this to me. She has a beautiful singing voice. She often takes off her muskrat stole and lays it on my lap so I can pinch its plastic clothespin mouth on my fingers, before she leaves the fifth pew to cricket her stockings up to the pulpit to move people with her rendition of "God Hath Not Promised" or "It Is Well with My Soul" or "Great Is Thy Faithfulness."

There is no music in her voice now. And her singing never has had anything to do with me.

"Talk to me. You must have been doing something you shouldn't have. 'Be sure your sins will find you out.' Remember that. God sees everything even when I am not there. It's not just me you are disappointing. You better go to bed, kneel down and ask Jesus for forgiveness. Have you ANYTHING to say?"

Yes. I have lots to say but my throat constricts. It hard to breathe. I certainly cannot talk. I feel sick to my stomach but ignore it. This time has been too close.

Maybe I could get pneumonia and go to the hospital again. I like it there, inside the clear plastic tent. I can really breathe in there. They pass little cups full of apple juice with straws, with crinkly bends in them to drink when you are lying down. It's a skill to do that without choking but I can. I have practised, lots.

The nurses are clean and white and cool. At bedtime they rub my back with lotion and sprinkle baby powder and tuck me in with an extra pillow to hug. They don't ask me any hard questions. I get to read little Golden Books or they read to me from the big storybook in the day room. I can sit in the sunroom listening to records too. I play Fish with the girl who broke her leg, but I put away the cards when I hear their footsteps on the brown linoleum.

"We don't play cards. They are bad." And they don't say why. I know not to ask them again.

~

Thirty-five years later, chalk poised on the blackboard, midway in a sentence about plot, I glimpse a Grade Ten girl as she tries to slip quietly into my English classroom after the bell has gone. We have a late policy, so I stop her before she gets through the door.

"Where were you?" I demand, elbows jutting akimbo. I notice the twig and leaf in her left running shoe. I notice her eyes. The image of my five-year-old self comes back to me.

I set the chalk gently on the ledge and ask the class to begin reading. I whisper quietly to her, "I was worried about you. Are you all right? Perhaps I can help?"

"No, not all right," comes the answer, and we go together to get her the help she needs.

Andrew Wade

KATIE, SISTER

Six years young, Katie wore
a bleached cotton sundress
with papier mâché over wire
hanger wings. It took thirty days,
eight newspapers, and one hair dryer
for me to set her feathers to form,
so she could welcome in the Baby Jesus.

"I need you. The beach spot."
A text. Katie. Fourteen years old.
I phoned back—no reply—left a party
mid-conversation, and let
my fifth-hand Chevy roar.

She had always been loved a little less, mistreated
a little more, some family cruelty I couldn't understand.

Katie gazed over the rioting ocean,
a hastily assembled backpack beside her
filled with clothes and lunches she never ate,
her skirted legs dangling from the rock face, kicking
pebbles loose with her heels, her toes reaching
for ground. She looked
like a ballerina torn
from her music box.
I wiped her mascara and put
my arm around her shoulders,
slender wishbones,
and led her away from the wind.
She fell asleep in the seat beside me,
knees tucked, arms askew at angles.
My coat covered her, chin to ankle.

We roomed together for a time,
her nuzzled into my couch or
pacing around my room. I found
all her new habits, good and ill,
the eggshells she'd keep from omelettes
and line them along the window sill,
a shelf of flightless birds.

She left
when they never asked about her,
took a Greyhound to Ontario,
left me a note, no number,
phones me every month or so,
promising to come back sometime,
but not any time soon.

Elee Kraljii Gardiner

THINGS I WOULD EXPLAIN TO YOU NOW

On Sunday mornings I hid in the closet
while you waited, hat in hand
on the stone steps—never crossing the doorsill—
to take us to the aquarium. My sisters waited, too, torn.
I fumed among the coats and galoshes:
stupid Persephone ate six of those
heart-red seeds; I'd made no such bargain.
Eventually I'd honour an exchange,
placate my two tall gods and give
myself over bravely,
eyes red, tom-girl heart thrashing beneath my ribs.
We never spoke of it,
my dread, I mean.
No one ever spoke of it, meaning
no one was ever blamed.

Nasstasia Yard

THE BOY WITH THE RED CRAYON

I didn't care
when he called me a slut
when he crayoned the windows in red:
 "one million men have entered your cunt"
and when
he gathered all my dresses
upon the balcony
and set them on fire
I didn't care
I felt nothing for him
and when
he encouraged me to saw with a blade
the thin membrane of skin
on my inner wrist
I didn't worry
when he chased me into
the alley
because I knew
I would be leaving
because I was practiced
at walking backwards and seeing
through the rear of my skull
while the inquisitor heckled me.

So when mom came to get me
in the pickup
and we threw
all my belongings
in the back
I saw his face,
revealed from behind
the inquisitor's mask,

drooping in shame
against the window
crayoned in red

I think I felt nothing for him
I hope that I felt nothing—
because I always thought
I was an exception
to that kind of abuse

Zhong M. Chen

GLARING GLASSES

Here is a real-life story originally told in Chinese by a woman who has chosen to remain anonymous for personal and cultural reasons. She has read the English translation and given me the permission to publish it.

It's been like this over the past decade, on and off. He would return at the crack of dawn, staggering up the stony stairs and stammering some gibberish from his foamed mouth, smacking of cigarettes and Chinese beers. He would fling his smoked clothes on the floor, shake his shoes off and pitter-patter to the washroom. Then came splashes of water and his euphoric singing, oblivious to all around him. I would have to get up and shush him down. Not every neighbour could put up with the randy and low noise.

He could afford to stay out late because he's the boss of his own company. He doesn't have to care about regular work schedules or an overworked body. He can sleep until midday, get up, eat something and sleep again. He can sleep for twelve hours on end. He's got a kingdom.

"I lost eighty thousand dollars overnight," he boasted the other day. "That's manly. I never even blinked an eye. That's Northerners' generosity."

I never checked. Money was my smallest concern then. He played mah-jong all night. "In my line of work, I've got to have connections. Dining and gaming and winning make good connections. I work hard at my work."

One time I struck out. Carrying my son on my back, I went straight to the gambling house—a house of his mah-jong partners. I yanked the door open and stood still in the middle of the doorway for a long, hard minute. The rustling and clacking of the mah-jong tiles were deafening; wet, black smoke poured out in plumes. All of a sudden, the rowdy crowd turned silent; all eyes moved towards me. I knew I had a commanding presence. He reluctantly stood up and walked towards me.

"Go home."

I did not budge. He repeated it, adding an exclamation mark. I said nothing and held my ground. He said it the third time. I retorted, "You, home." I swung around and stormed out. Just as the doors were fanning towards me, I heard someone say, "What a young beauty professor you've got, man." Utter silence reigned.

He did stop going gambling at night for a while. Then one day, I got a call from the police: "Your husband's run into a tree. The car's totalled." I rushed to the hospital, only to discover he was just fine, and fully capable of inflicting further insult upon injuries: "You are to blame. Your harsh criticism drove me mad, drove me to drinking, to drunk driving, to death almost." I recalled that a day or two ago, when food I made was not to his taste, he pulled a long face and said, "Why didn't you buy something fresher and cut the veggies finer?"

"Do it yourself."

He did it. He drove himself into a tree. I bought myself life insurance the next day. I refused to be dragged into the death trap. I took precautious measures.

He promised never to do it again, again and again. He knelt down on the hard floor when he was sober, he wrote repentant letters, he made solemn oaths. I couldn't bear seeing a man down on his knees begging for pardon, and forgave him. The scene repeated time and again.

Sometimes, if he did not have enough drinking pals, he would wash himself, eat something nutritious and sit down comfortably on the large sofa to watch TV, all the time waiting for me to finish my studies or preparing for work. If I did this past two, he would say, "Don't stay up. It's already late." After I wrapped up my task, took a shower and got ready to sleep, he would come up and say, "I want it."

"Not tonight."

"I want it."

"Not tonight. It's two already and I have to get up at six."

"You're my wife. I have the right, don't I?"

He's unusually strong, heavy and big. I knew he would insist until he got it; he's got all the time and energy. Better to get it done with. I relented, though resenting. His cigarette-smelling and beer-saturated mouth tried to find mine, but I averted it by turning and twisting my head and neck. He did this and that with insatiable appetite and tormented me for two hours until something exploded. Satisfied, he dropped to a snoring slumber as if nothing else existed.

I needed a shower. I looked at his roaring body again, and I struggled to stand up. I dropped to the side and fell to sleep immediately in spite of myself. I woke up with puffy eyes and a swimming head. But my students were waiting. I packed up and went to teach without a breakfast. My dark, bushy hair started to fall off and thin out. I used to be a picture of health, youth and wealth. Now I am not. Who can save me? Who can salvage me? I've always wondered.

Last summer I ran into John, a man of an uncanny sense of things hidden and bursting to come out. He got me talking. His big, bright and beautiful eyes pierced through his glasses; they were an inviting ocean for things to flow into. I blurted out my stories, one at a time, at different times. After several of these, he still urged me to tell more, to tell it all. At the end, his eyes would flare up and encourage me to do something. He said so and wrote, "What the hell are you doing with your life? Why hush up the stories? Tell, yell, tell him to go to hell." It's destiny that I met John. He changed my life.

When home, I started to tell, I started to yell. I told *him* to go to hell. "If you die drinking and driving, you deserve it. My son and I won't go with you. You think you just smashed a side of the tree? You could've easily harmed or killed others. You already damaged a big tree. You think a big tree doesn't feel? I am not going that way with you."

The decent Chinese community frowned on smoking, drinking, gambling— any one of these vices. He had them all. The only thing missing was wooing women or hiring prostitutes, but he had me for his libidinal outlet with a vengeance. I had to stop him on his slippery slope.

Then last August he came back late, and stoned as usual. He yelled loudly, "Get up and pick up the broken glass." I woke up, put on my pyjamas and rushed out, afraid he might wake up my son or the neighbours. I did what I was told to. My son came out of his room, too. As my son and I wrestled with millions of pieces of a broken wine bottle, a sliver of glass pricked my index finger. Red blood streaked out. My son darted over to stop the blood. My husband remained motionless on the huge sofa, smelly, smoked and stoned. Under the bright ceiling light, the shards on the hard, cold stone floor metamorphosed into small mirrors shining on my dishevelled hair, haggard face and streaming eyes. On a big piece of glass, I saw my own face: a university professor with my due pride in my profession. My students have commented on my grace and elegance in the classroom; my colleagues have said the same outside the classroom. I could not reconcile their image of me with what I saw of myself now, picking up broken bits of a drunkard's glass bottle one by one and my glasses. I saw John's bright and glaring eyes and glasses, too. All of these images forced a new message upon me. The shimmering contrast was too much.

I also felt family duties and chores weighing heavily on me. Chinese moral code demands wifely duties to the husband, to the idea of a family, to my son. I would have rather he had an affair, or affairs, so that I would have an excuse to seek a divorce. I am a chicken by the Chinese zodiac. I always returned home by the evening. He seldom worried that I would stay out late. He had said so to his drinking and dining pals, who told me in his absence. "You are a good wife and mother," they said that almost in unison, bobbing their heads like buoys in the bubbling sea of beers and bread.

A familiar scene came back to me. When sober, he seemed to repent each time. He bought many gifts to soothe me, or rather, to shut me up: clothes, clothes and clothes. Thirty-thousand dollars worth, he said proudly one day. Then he asked, are they enough? Then another sight flashed before me like a frame of film: shattered bits and pieces of the TV screen scattered all over the place. He had no regrets about it. "If old things don't go, new things won't come. I have money."

I told John the stories over the phone. He gave me good and timely advice again on entrenched patterns of behaviour and strategies to deal with them. I could visualize his clear and clean eyes and glasses. I needed to take effective actions. And I did.

One day, when my son forgot to come to eat supper with us at a restaurant, my husband smashed his face into a bloody pulp. Our son had not turned thirteen yet then. How could a young kid understand or remember all the rules and chores all the time? A slip of memory did not deserve so much abuse, so much violence, so much swearing and cursing, so much blood shed. A thirteen-year-old's brain is still developing and deserves some allowance for mistakes. He replied, "He's my son, too, and I have every right to hit him, the stinking little son." I worried about the scars on his young face. What girl would like a scarred face? There are so many more boys than girls now, with everyone wanting a son in a family. The odds are piling up against or rather, in my son's face. He might grow new skin, though. I hope.

I yelled, "Why so much violence? You're a brute!"

He replied, "He's my son, my stinking little son. If I don't punish him, who will?" He swaggered away.

After the hitting incident, he returned home with a big fish and meaty crabs. "See, I bought them to nourish you two." My son and I kept silent. We had formed a united front without knowing it. Snubbed, my husband went about mopping the floor, his self-chosen task of regret or repentance.

I couldn't believe it. Two months later, when he did badly on an exam, my son said to me, "Don't hit my head." I asked, "Where should I hit?" "Hit my bum, Mom, my bum." I was speechless. He'd just celebrated his thirteenth birthday. John said that an abusive pattern appeared in me now. I'd better watch out.

When he hit our son and drew blood, I suggested a divorce. He said he would never agree to that. I said to myself, when the time is ripe, it is not for you to decide.

Now I said this to him, "Smoking is harmful to our son, to me and to you. You know that." He replied: "A man is a man when he smokes. In the North, even women take pride in smoking."

"Why should you follow and defend bad habits?" I said, repeating what John had noted, adding, "You must not smoke inside our house."

A week into the new year of 2010, my son called my mom and proudly said, "My mom is now the boss of the house. She gives orders and reprimands whenever she likes. How come your daughter is like that?" I heard my mom reply, half in jest, "That's not the daughter I've known."

On my desk, my new pair of glasses glared gladly back.

Sonia Di Placido

THE WARM EMBRACE OF WRECKAGE

How do you get out of this fucked-up pattern? How do you leave behind the one person that has made you so dependent to the point where you don't believe in yourself anymore? You hate yourself and you hate them. And you might say, "Yes, I love you, and I'm loving myself," but what's really going on is the twist, the paradox that what's so, so, so good, can be so, so, so bad.

I wanted a daddy that would give me the world and I didn't get it. Instead, I became the first-born son, and in me grew the warrior child. I was also a girl who became an angry woman. I went out into the world a roaring wolf. Later I met the lamb in myself—only to discover what it means to fall. Yes. Fall in love—crucify one's self. I fell in love and it turned into utterly horrible words, words, words, insults and passionate rages.

We separated. He married. He went to therapy. Four years later I was still alone and struggling to be independent. I'd become more of a grieving lamb that had lost a father. What I saw in the man I thought I had loved before was really my deeper psyche's quest to attain what I hadn't received. He took care of me emotionally when I was out of control because I had been suffering. Both of us were suffering, yet unable to see what the other person saw; our communication crumbled.

Five years later I met someone new. He gave me attention, he desired me and I brought him into my home. Quick and desperate, we came together for better or worse. But within three months I was kept against my will, raped, held at knifepoint and told, "If you make a move, I'll cut your throat." I cried and begged. I knew I'd become a lamb to the wolf. A reversal had taken place; I was no longer that daring idealist wolf with ambitions. I had fallen for a charming illusion; he had ties to the drug trade, cocaine and the world of organized crime.

I did not know how to get help. Too afraid to call the police, feeling responsible and entirely at fault, I gave up. My parents blamed me and responded in two extremes: hysterics from Mama and cool aloofness from Papa. "Can't help. You should know better. Get rid of him. We're leaving town." By the time I'd got some help from two caring friends, my grandparents were all I had and they were both fragile: mentally ill and suffering from bad relationship patterns themselves. They spent the majority of their lives engaged in irrational arguments and suffering bitter anguish over one another. They were unable to acknowledge their own mistakes and understand that holding grudges wouldn't do. They were stubborn and self-righteous. My family had a history of doomed relationships. My own, my parents', my grandparents'. So, before my friends offered their support to me, I thought to myself, "If this is what I am meant for, then this is where I'll stay. In hell with this man, this brute with a history of violence." I gave up. I gave in. This is what culture can do.

I hardly knew what was buried underneath and how it was linked directly to the issues of my own cultural past and the relationships I'd seen before me; my parents, my grandparents, the peasant Italian influences and background. And for a time I believed I shouldn't leave because it was my fault. It was sad and extreme but he really needed me. I believed he really loved me. Traditionally, in my culture, women would have no choice. She would be expected to support her spouse, be loyal to the end, even at her own peril and at the risk of her own salvation.

But today, in western society, I found a different sort of friend, someone with a different point of view and independence, both emotional and financial, who offered a new kind of learning. I found a surprise rescue from a high school girlfriend with a planned program to get me out. We met in a park. I was clueless and she divulged her concerns about me through tears. She asked me to return to the house where her parents and boyfriend were waiting; we could call the police. I froze. I told her I couldn't—that I was trapped. He would kill me. But her genuine assurance and advice to just return to the house was enough and within a few hours on a Saturday afternoon on a mid-July day, we called the Women's Helpline.

A few days later I reached out to another friend and explained that I was alone, safe to get help, get away and call the police. I stole his passport. I stole identification. I took everything that was necessary to get out for an afternoon and I put on the sweetest lie, the loveliest smile before he left my apartment. He looked at me and noticed there was something different and he said, "See, I wish you could be so sweet to me like this all the time, then we wouldn't have to fight." We parted with a kiss. I watched him walk away from the balcony and that was the last time I ever saw him. After the initial charges were pressed; the detective and I planned an arrest and restraining order.

The trial never happened because he was bailed out of jail by his family, and he escaped without ever appearing for his pre-trial hearings; he must have left the country but to this day I still do not know. A warrant for his arrest remains a decade later. My case sits cold with a bench warrant. And I couldn't bring myself to claim for criminal-injuries compensation until recently. The work meant revisiting and reliving it all over again and I wanted to put it on hold. It was far too painful, so much paperwork and I was tired, exhausted, overwhelmed.

I can't trust anyone not to hurt me anymore, and after three abusive relationships with different kinds of abuse—verbal, physical or emotional—if someone so much as comes too close, where does my love go? What love have I got left to give? I know I'll only hurt them because I am broken, broken, broken. A thunderstorm, a tornado moving over the terrain of this earth; an angry destroyer wanting to attack for what has been done to me.

Love me. Love me. Love me. Please. Love me and don't. Don't. Stay away. Keep away. I don't need you. But I desperately need you because I am afraid of finding some peace. Is there peace?

It's been over ten years since I pressed charges and I am still working through this. The battered-woman story is so passé today—that's how I feel most of the time. It's a story that's more than a thousand years old and we all know it. Why bother fighting it? I've got the pain in my body, pent up in memory, no matter how much spinning, how much yoga, how many antidepressants and how much therapy. How many tears will it take?

Wendy Donawa

SPELL TO BANISH GHOSTS

Creak open the heart's
cumbersome travelling trunk.
Unfold the stained fabric.
Rotten threads give way
in the unsound weave.
Dismay sours the air,
fouls the lungs,
fear's spoor thick in the throat.

The waste   the waste
hurtling endlessly down
the mind's garbage chute.
Turn from it.
Turn from it.

Know lakewater
lying calm in the evening light.
Know the road's chicory-spangled verge,
granite peaks austere in the cold heights.
Know moonflood in the room,
candleshine darting in
the small silver tray,
the celadon pot
centring the shelf,
centring the self.

Love, take heart.
Heart, take love.

Elee Kraljii Gardiner

VANCOUVER, STILL LIFE

The rain line drips at the alley's mouth
     two figures against the wall
     curl their shoulders in conference
     this intimacy
     is all it takes
     to conjure a curtain of privacy
     despite cars fuming a yard away
     he unlaces her boot
     baring luminous ankle
     the taper of her foot
     —such tenderness
     in an ugly place—
     he raises his hand
     to the light and twirls
     his wrist, all delicacy and art
     a bubble refracts
     street light, raindrop, glint
     of the hungry eye
     she turns her face
     to the neon, a sweet thing
     that blue light
     catches the scabs and bruises
     of her face, a topography of collision
     the leg of her jeans
     is slack with soak
     her laces drawl
     and she thrusts her foot forward
     insisting on the kiss of a syringe
     the rain strikes with little fingers
     need glitters here
     and if he is brusque with the belt
     it's because she is beyond the bricks
     and he has a habit of chasing her

Susan Musgrave

HEROINES

Question:
Have you been hurt by men,
have you been raped?

I've been raped, yes,
but what hurts worse is the way
they look at you afterwards
when they refuse to pay

as if you're the one dirty habit
they can't break.

Fathers
I've had my share—a real one
who went to Toronto to quit drinking,
he said when he came back we'd be
a family again but he never came back.
Adopted fathers, foster fathers,
group-home fathers and one I was sent to
to confess my sins. I grew up thinking
a man's knee was something you sat
naked on, something I should be

grateful for. I try to imagine a world
where someone is grateful for anything.

The father I hated best? The one who
paid me for sex. We lived on a farm
and if I said no to him he threatened
to kill one of my favourite pets,
some maimed creature, a runt I'd

raised myself until it grew strong enough
to fend for itself; he told me I'd be next.
I'd go with him, early, before daylight
to feed the animals and do the things
he told me to do, down on my knees.

Now when I'm pulling a date,
I'm not really there, I'm doing what
I wanted to do when I was growing up.
I wanted to be an animal trainer, to
train animals to run and keep running
forever, like some wild part of me
no one can ever touch.

Childhood

One time the man who calls himself our father
made me crawl to him on a carpet of broken
glass. There are days I feel
as old as the Bible he makes me read;

he says it's a good book, full of lessons
I have to learn, like when to bend
over our father's knee and let his fingers
enter me because I have sinned; one time
for seven days he made me lie in a grave
with the dog I let out of the yard next door;
he got run over by the man who beat him
every day—I'd just wanted to help that dog
get away. The father said I should pray
and I do but it don't change much of anything.
The dog never gets his life back no matter
how long I lie there, naked and ashamed
of myself, beside him.

I remember the sound of the skin being sliced
from my body, of glass cutting bone. Even when
he entered me I wasn't allowed to cry,
crying was for babies not girls like me.
I tore, but I wouldn't bleed. Over and over

again I was torn but I wouldn't bleed,
and I don't think he ever forgave me
for holding out on him.

Spare Me

After he had me there would be blood
on the bedspread, all over the sheets,
I got so used to it I didn't think
you could have sex without blood, the two
went together, like grief and laughter
they had a joined-at-the-hip relationship,
the kind I had with the rooster my foster dad
kept tied by one leg to the bedpost in the
spare room where I slept. It was called
the spare room even though it had been
my room ever since I had come to live
with them on the farm, spare as in extra,
spare as in not very much. The rooster got less
than I did, a dish of water he shit in
as if to let them know what he thought
of the treatment he got. A few seeds,
hardly enough, he scattered all over the
rug; I learned not to ask how's he supposed
to eat with his beak tied shut. My father would
only say spare me the grief.

The rooster had flown at him once,
ripping his face, then tearing around
the yard like a chicken with his head cut off
(my foster mother said) and spitting out
my father's tough lips by the pig trough.
Killing him would be too quick, my father said,
there were worse things than death,
and so he, too, was spared
and made to live.

Bad Date

The whole time I never stop
looking him in the eye, he wants me

to cry or beg but I won't give him
the satisfaction. I just fix
onto his eyes, all the time working
to get my hands free; duct tape is like
everything—it's got a lifespan.
He rapes me, sticks a gun down my throat
and sodomizes me, but nothing he does
gets a rise out of me. Not until he burns me,
flicking matches onto my skin where they stick
and I smell my own flesh burning
do I break: I sweat, I start to shake
and then a tear I can't stop slips down
my face—just one—that's all
it takes, he knows I am his.

He's given me a taste, am I ready
to eat? I tell him if I'm hungry
I'll eat, there's nothing
that doesn't belong to me.

The poems in the sequence "Heroines" were drawn from the stories of six women, heroin-addicted prostitutes, from Vancouver's Downtown Eastside. Director Stan Feingold commissioned the poems as a "script" for his documentary film, Heroines *(2001). The sequence was published as* Mother's Day Behind the West Hotel *in a limited edition chapbook from Poetgoat Press.*

Yvonne Blomer

ABANDONED SHOE, RUE ST. CATHÉRINE

It's new, wooden, a clog,
leather strapped. Flash of
painted toe nail, and foot,
shoeless, stumbling away,
body, off-kilter, following or
woman caught, being pulled
into a car as it pulls away—
she could be laughing, or drunk,
could have a hand, sticky
with sweat, held fast, over
her open mouth.

Anne Hopkinson

A NUMBER OF WOMEN ARE MISSING

She stood before the podium and called to one
And all the people gathered there for these two
Dead women who walked the streets at three
In the morning never to return, so that by four
In the afternoon the neighbours made teams of five
Who searched, and were filmed for the news at six.

Added to the missing women, now the six
Of them named and photographed one by one,
Reporters interviewed the parents and partners in five
Minute segments, broadcast on channel two
To all corners of the city, a warning for
The population: one hundred to the power of three.

And prayers were prayed to the holy three,
Candles lit and placed together for the six
Women of the tribes and nations, from the four
Closest reservations, and not a word or hint, no one
Said his name, or his friend's name, the deadly two,
In for eight years for assault and rape, out after five.

Children called indoors for safety by five
O'clock, checking the gate and the locks three
Times to be sure. Take a drink or two
For edgy nerves, it's like rolling double six
Boxcars, and feeling crapped out, still alert at one
A.m. as the horsemen come riding in a line of four.

A year they lay buried for the four
Seasons of decay, beneath five
Feet of mud and rock under a one
Metre wide path, where he walked maybe three
Times a day, from patio to garden plot, to water his six
Tomato plants, eating one or two

Fresh, as he thought how he had killed two
On the same day, how he was still hot and jumpy for
Their fear. And already a stirring, a sixth
Sense reminded him it only took five
Seconds to drag another bitch into his three
Year old blue van, not too clean, not too dirty, so no one

Ever looked closely, or remembered how one
Slut was there and then gone. Two, three, four,
Five, six of them, the first half dozen.

Madeleine Nattrass

SOME MEASURE OF FREEDOM *

Crouch behind his sick fantasies
as he cruises the strip
singles out his prey
makes his move
stabs his hate
smothers reason
dumps it in a farmer's field.

Daughters, mothers, sisters
become black dots on a map.
How to trace the circumference of this madness.

* *Appeal court dashes sex-killer's dream of moving to less secure facility in hopes of meeting women. The ruling creates a roadblock to a steady trickle of psychopathic killers who have been applying for transfers based on solid good conduct records making it difficult to deny a transfer or some measure of freedom.*

—*Kirk Makin,* Globe and Mail, *May 17, 2006.*

Jessica Michalofsky

SOME POEMS NEVER GET WRITTEN

Because they pass out. Because they fellatio constellation. Because they cervical cancer condom machine. Because they shoot pool lurid. Because they can't remember the names. Because they last call over and over. Because they hitch-hike. Because they remember, and they don't like it. Because they susceptibility ratio. Because they obituary. Because they're too high. Because sometimes it feels good. Because for the first hour, they lifetime, they green span, they daughter, they rainstorm, they orgasm, they red leaves, they cat, they soft fur, they coins in pocket, they new born, they kaleidoscope, they cello, they big sky. Because after that, they cold teeth, they grind, they flat, they socket, they burn spot, they ashtray, they hustle, they more. Because they didn't ever come home. Because they left children. Because they are shadowy and sometimes I catch glimpses. Because they look just like me. Because they left their photographs in my wallet. Because they bought me draft beer. Because they hair braid. Because they peed in the alleys. Because they laughed outrageously. Because they borrowed my gold dress and looked fantastic. Because they were more beautiful. Because they dead. Because I am living.

Janet Marie Rogers

IN WALKS CHARLIE

I was bottoming out. I made a bad drinker but that didn't stop me from consuming excessive amounts of alcohol most nights of the week, only to wake up wishing there was a loaded gun on the bedside table. I was in a relationship with an abusive man from which I could find no exit. It was 1990. My Mohawk brothers and sisters were defending their land in Kanesatake. I managed to get a job with the City of Toronto Public Works Department as a street cleaner that year. Otherwise I would've joined the standoff to contribute my confused version of support.

The job was a humble means to make a living. The union ensured we made a very decent wage for keeping the streets clean, but I was still a mess. That first year, on the days I made it to work, I'd arrive hung right over, sometimes sporting a shiner. The makeup I applied could no better hide the bruised eye than the lame excuses I made to keep people away from the truth. I kept at the job though. The paycheque helped soothe the humiliation.

I had a beat that took me along Queen West, Parkdale side. Three-quarters of the way through my shift, I'd stop in to the Parkdale Library for a bathroom break and to kill some time. On my fourth or fifth visit, I found a parapsychology book called *Strangers Among Us* by Ruth Montgomery misshelved in the biography section. The book was always there every time I returned, waiting for me to read another section. It explained that walk-ins were spirit beings from other planes who make mutual contracts to enter the bodies of humans so they can do good on this earth plane without having to go through the growing-up stages. It went on to say they usually worked in normal blue-collar jobs such as store clerks, truck drivers or street cleaners.

There was a man at work I was getting to know. His name was Charlie and he'd say the strangest things. He talked about biblical times as if he was there, and how giants used to walk the earth. He was a strong unionist, and rallied the other employees to participate in union matters that would result in their best interest. He said he was a Maritimer hailing from Nova Scotia. Charlie was a rock.

He arrived to work one day wearing a Band-Aid on the side of his nose. He'd had a large mole removed. After two days, the Band-Aid was gone and so was any trace of a scar or any medical procedure whatsoever. Each time I read a chapter in the book, I felt I was being given clues as to who Charlie really was. The book mentioned that most walk-ins have severe problems with addictions—Charlie's was alcohol. He'd drink amounts that would blind most people and still be able to walk away.

Charlie knew the state I was in. I believe it was in his contractual obligations to assist me. He made cryptic comments like "Do you smell the bread? Can you hear the trumpets? Let it go." He told me I'd write something someday that would bring me notoriety. At the time, I dreamed of a career in the visual arts. One of the first places I showed my work was at a fundraising auction for the Oka Defence Fund. Charlie was there lending his support for the cause. His excitement influenced the other bidders, creating a frenzy around my felt-pen piece titled "Recipe for the Future," which sold for $314 dollars.

After working with the city for a year, I quit drinking and doing drugs. I'm pleased to say I have been clean and sober for nineteen years now. So how does this prove Charlie is a walk-in?

It was Christmas and my mother had made the trek from Hamilton to visit me. She has psychic skills, so I bugged her to give me a reading. Among other things, she tapped into a man who she said was not very attractive and who also was not from here. She said this man would give me a box where I could put my wishes, and that she could see this man working on this box, putting energy into it.

The following weekend, I had people over for a holiday gathering and Charlie presented me with carved wooden sculptures of birds, a male and a female. When the carvings are flipped on their backs, a sliding panel is revealed which opens to a pocket inside the birds. Charlie explained I was to write my wishes down and put them inside.

It only took a couple of years after starting my job with the city for my life to spin around. I moved away from the bruiser who later died from a drug overdose, left the city job and began working in arts administration. Two years after that, I moved from Toronto to Victoria and two years after that, I began writing.

Writing consumes me now. I've shared my writing all over the world, and my spoken-word tracks have been included on national compilation recordings.

Charlie once told me that religion is nothing more than putting something back from where it came. He stood by my bookshelf, removed a book and put it back to demonstrate the simplicity of his statement. I later remembered the mis-shelved book in the library. I took a photo of Charlie at the Labour Day parade that I keep on my wall. The photo fell one day, so I picked it up and put it back. It fell again. That's when I knew Charlie was practising his religion—and returning.

Bharat Chandramouli

LOVING A SURVIVOR

Interview by Emma Cochrane

Who is the survivor close to you?

The survivor in this case is my long-time partner and my story is based on the many years that I've spent with her, talking to her and having her experiences shared from her to me. As I think about it, I look back to how far she and I have come in our knowledge of sexual violence. The first time we talked about it, the most obvious thing to do would have been to actually tell someone or to get support and we didn't do that. We've thought about how much education has helped.

How long ago was it when you first began talking about her abuse? How long has this journey been?

Maybe thirteen or fourteen years.

What did you know about sexualized violence before you met her?

Not much but I knew it existed. I knew it was something that every woman had to be worried about because I saw it on TV, saw it on the streets, saw it every day. But it's not something that we, as men—or anyone—are given any tools to deal with. We didn't know what to do when confronted with that. The only thing we knew—or that I knew—was that it happened to all the women in your life. And it was always the outsiders, the people on the street, the people in the bus, the people in the cinema theatre who would hassle your sisters, your cousins and your parents, whoever it was. For me it was always the stranger, outsider, not my kind of person, who would be inflicting violence.

It was really about what women could do to avoid the situation and as men, or boys, we knew you shouldn't do things like that. And if you saw something like that happening to your friends or your family, you were supposed to just get them away from the situation. I think the dialogue between the women was more about the precautions you needed to take because this could happen or that could happen. But it was always framed as a bunch of don'ts: don't dress immodestly; don't look up, look down; don't ever make eye contact; don't go out at night; don't go out alone.

That's all I knew besides what was shown in the media and on TV and all that. Movies pretty much only showed women in sexual situations when they were getting assaulted. I mean that was it. And then a bad thing would always happen to them half an hour later—they'd kill themselves or something like that. We thought, it happens to other people and when it happens it's a horrible thing. It was as if we were told to just avoid it and not talk about it.

How did you learn about sexualized violence from your partner?

We'd just been on a few dates. Nothing serious at that point. I think something came up in conversation that was similar to a situation that she had either very recently encountered, or it had only recently stopped or it was still happening. So she told me about this abuse that was happening to her.

The abuse was by a close family member, somebody that I knew. It was very shocking—well, I wouldn't say shocking because it's too generic of an emotion. It was a complicated mix of emotions.

I had no clue how to respond to something like that or what to do or how to be there, or how to support her. All I could say was "I hear you and I'm listening." When she told me we basically decided that I would look out for her in that situation, which was, again, strange. How could I? I didn't know what to do.

We discussed whether we wanted to tell anyone. And at that point in time, she felt we couldn't because she was living in a functioning household. Telling would have involved breaking up her family—or that's what we thought at that point in time. So we didn't know what to do. We didn't do anything. We just decided on a set of precautions that she would take to ensure that it would never happen again, which it didn't. Basically, that was it. I said, I'll be there, I'll listen. As far as our relationship goes, it doesn't matter at all. What we have is what we have. What happened there we can deal with later.

Eventually, she told her family. Eventually the person involved in this was exposed to her family, the people in her life that she was most afraid it would hurt. It hurt them in completely different ways.

Her family is still completely intact. Nothing's changed there—only the support has increased. So a lot of her fears did not come true.

But that's beside the point.

How did learning about your partner's experience change your perception of sexualized violence?

It didn't at first. But I went back home and thought about it and then I realized that I had heard things like this happening before. It's just that it was never discussed. Once you hear one story, you start thinking about snippets of half-stories you heard in your life and start making sense of those.

I grew up in a family where I was the youngest by far, so I was always the least spoken to about these kinds of situations. But I heard things. And then, only then, I made sense of certain cryptic statements that I'd always hear like, "He's strange," or "Oh, yeah, he likes having girls on his lap," or "He looks at you strangely." You hear all these things as a kid and they just kind of go over your head most of the time because as a boy I wasn't exposed to that kind of abuse or those kinds of behaviours from anyone. For the first few years of being with my partner, nothing really did blow my mind or change a lot of the ways I thought about sexualized violence, but I was still young.

It was just a blip in our lives, I thought, because we were both young and this person I was dating was a super strong, confident, young person, on the verge of getting out of there, of leaving and doing other things. To me, it seemed like, yeah, it happened; at some point in time, he's going to have to pay, but maybe this is not that time. And it'll be over, it'll be in the past—like you fractured your leg or something.

It didn't feel it was something that was going to take a long time to heal. I had no clue. I didn't know the words "post-traumatic stress disorder" at that point in time.

Later on, you began to notice certain triggers. Can you talk about those triggers?

Well, then we got hitched and we moved in together and it coincided with a lot of changes in her life and mine. We were suddenly in a different country, we didn't know that many people, she didn't know anyone. And there were some other medical reasons. She got depressed. It wasn't quickly, but it happened a few months after we moved. That changed our dynamic quite a bit. During her depression, in the last few months before she went into any kind of therapy, she would have these strange flashbacks. We would ascribe them to various incidents that happened in the past, including the abuse. But, again, it was more of a "that's only happening because you're already depressed" kind of thing.

She went into therapy. One of the first things that came out in therapy was the abuse. Over a year or two, the therapist started digging, and once the therapist started digging, our interaction got really difficult. She was going through a really tough time because she'd always been a super high-flyer, extremely outgoing, very confident and suddenly it was all gone.

She was going through a very hard time. I was trying my best trying to understand what was going on, and trying to help, obviously. But my help was me trying to problem solve, which in hindsight, is not always wise.

But you do what you do. You have to learn, right? So, the therapeutic process got a lot of these things out at a time when I don't know if she was ready for it. I think I've learned over the years that different therapy regimens have different approaches. Some therapists just say we have to deal with getting some of your basic stuff back together, and then we can deal with some of the more hairy stuff later, but these first few years, when she was going through it, was more about addressing the abuse first.

So there were a lot of flashbacks, a lot of triggers, a lot of unpleasantness for her, and I guess for me as well. It was hard for me to frame it as being unpleasant for me, but it was. It was a lot of stress, even though I understood what was happening.

That's kind of where my education started. We would talk about the therapy and how it was going, and if she needed to talk about it, or talk to somebody else about it. I went to counselling for a while, off and on and on and off. I was in the middle of grad school and I wasn't going forward. I felt I was doing this great, worthy thing; I'm helping this wonderful person get better and heal. I thought I should be spending all of my energy doing that. And yeah, my schoolwork suffered.

Once I went to therapy, I quickly realized that the way you help is by taking care of what you're supposed to do, and always be aware that you need to live your life. The best way to help a survivor is to just be there and let them deal with it at their own pace, let them work through it, however long that takes. I needed to take a more hands-off approach. That's been the constant struggle and it's always, for me, a shifting pendulum of problem solving versus not problem solving, and being very attached versus being more supportive and independent. I have not won that battle.

What would you tell other men about supporting survivors?

Listen and be patient. Don't try to take charge. Don't problem solve. Be a partner through the journey, not a leader. Don't try to take things into your hands. Don't try to beat people up. If she or he wants to report it, let them do it. If they don't, let it be. But obviously the most important thing you can do right away is get both of you out into a safe place.

It needs to stop right away if it's happening. That's the first thing. There's no compromise. If it's at work, then you have to leave. If it's a relative, then you have to stop it. You have to make it stop first. Then, and only then, can you deal with the rest of it. That's the only time that you need to be very urgent and aggressive.

And if your partner is not able to do it, somehow the situation needs to be made safe. Then after that, step back.

I have been surprised that I was able to deal with it, and that's always something I feel good about. But I think how shocking it is that it takes a person that strong that long to get back on the rails after something that happened fifteen years ago. Hopefully, that path is not as tortuous for some people as it is for others. But I greatly respect what a survivor goes through as they transition from victim.

What works well in supporting your partner? What did you feel were good moments?

You know, I think we were both very analytical, so our good moments always came out of some shared psychological breakthrough that we got from someone we talked to, or a book we read, or something like that. To us, the good moments were realizing that it was mostly an individual journey, and that it needed to be done.

Another good moment came when one of her therapists actually said, "We're not going to deal with it [the abuse], I know that's your problem, but your bigger problem is that you're in a strange country and you don't have a job, you don't go to school. That's not going to work."

We kind of thought, ah-ha, and she just concentrated on getting the basic building blocks of life back together. And I think when she started volunteering, helping others get through domestic violence—shelters, hotlines, and she signed up to do crisis-line volunteer training— she really started a big learning process for both of us.

At first I thought, this is nuts, you cannot do this, you can't be serious. Why are you putting yourself through this? But in hindsight, I was very proud of the fact that she basically didn't listen to me. She knew a lot about violence and women's issues and a lot of the language around it: the basics, the structure, how violence happens, how it's about power.

That's when my thinking around a lot of these issues evolved. Learning for the first time was really cool.

What do you think you learned about prevention? What tools do you see at our disposal?

I think with some men the big issue is a lack of knowledge, a lack of the tools to recognize quickly that something was happening, and deal with it right away.

I wish something as basic as this was given in our education. Just basic education. Comprehensive sexual education is one of the best ways to deal with that kind of situation.

Also, there's the very unequal status between men and women in society, and ideas about what men and women can do. The more you blur gender distinctions, the less stereotyping we do of male and female gender characteristics, the better it is for everyone. We were raised very strongly gendered. That gender stereotyping needs to go. Some people can break out of it—I did. I did a lot of "boy" things, but I was also interested in a lot of "girl" things.

Have other men ever talked to you about supporting survivors?

No, none of the men in my life. Either they have perfect lives, or they're not comfortable talking about it. So no, it's not happening. I'm hoping it's the former. It's not something that comes easily anyway. There's a lot of shame and stigma, especially in Indian culture. There's still a lot of shame and stigma.

Has this experience changed the way you thought about sexualized violence?

I used to call myself a feminist; now I think I am one. Ten, fifteen years ago I thought sexual violence abuse was a systemic issue. I've since learned that it's very structural, it's related to power, it's primarily men's use of power over women. In general, if the status of women in any society improves, violence will decrease as well.

That's one of the macro things I've learned, but on a micro level, you always have to speak up, and you always have to fight certain masculine tendencies—not within yourself, but amongst your peer group. You always have to listen to what other people have to say around you because you're probably hearing something you shouldn't be hearing and you need to use opportunities to say something.

I went to school with thirty boys and five girls. My undergraduate program had 270 men and 10 girls. The amount of pure frustration—just craziness related to lack of interaction, the amount of hate, hate speech, the amount of abusive language that was used around the women was just shocking. But I didn't do anything about it. I didn't know what to do.

As I've grown older, and as I move to different places, the language has become more subtle but the hate is still there, the stereotyping is still there, the abuse is still there. I'm learning to listen to that, learning to speak up and learning to break any language down to why it's happening and how I can do something about it. So I've learned quite a bit on a personal level.

In this journey with my partner, my perception of sexualized violence went from being something strange people did to the people you love to something that could happen anywhere to anyone at any place. And sexual violence not a product of sexual desire, but power and exercise of power. Sex is just a tool; it was not always the main point of why these things happen. And I finally understood how something like this could even take ten to fifteen years out of the life of someone, even someone who is as strong, smart and well-educated, able to deal with things, and as knowledgeable and analytical as my partner is. And that is very scary. You know someone who has all the abilities and all the tools to deal with it, and it is still taking that long. It's a life-long process.

Also, I learned that while you can help people get through, help them survive, help them deal with it after the fact, it's best not to ever let it happen.

Susan Braley

IN DEFENCE OF TREASURE

Every nation has been invited by the Norwegian government to place its seeds in
this vault. It's the last line of defence against extinction…and the most long-lasting,
most futuristic and most positive contribution to humanity being made by the
international community today. … [The vault's] design is as awesome physically as
it is attractive aesthetically, and both are fitting tributes to the importance of the
biological treasure to be stored there.
—*Dr. Carey Fowler, Global Crop Diversity Trust (2008–09), on the Svalbard Global*
Seed Vault.

In ordinary circumstances
the guard in the prison-orange parka might have been aroused
by the rising steam,
the titanic tunnel-mouth, held open,
at long last ready to receive.
But the mouth's not soft,
it's rimmed with frost, lashed
to an arctic mountain with metal and concrete.
Here, a Nordic angel Gabriel, the guard stands aside
as hooded white men drive immaculate packages
to twin chambers deep within. All species hallowed originals,
chosen ones, who, after catastrophe, will wake and save the world.
Every seed swaddled in four-fold laminate, catalogued
and tucked inside plastic pods with cherished others of its kind.
Now the donors withdraw, heads bowed in awe
at their embryonic Eden, made to replace the one they'll exhaust.
They seal their brave new world with steel doors,
not one, not two, but three;
set its dark portal ashimmer with prisms and mirrors,
a high-tech spectacle to rival the northern lights.
They step back then, chests lifted, and sing:

Blessed be rice from Asia, for it will be the seed of rising suns
Blessed be barley from Ethiopia, for it will sustain us with bread and beer
Blessed be matama from Mali, for it will grow where rain won't fall
Blessed be the soybean from China, for it will grow where rain won't cease
Blessed be the lentil from Lebanon, for it will be our poor man's meat
Blessed be wild banana from Honduras, for it will teach the sterile one to breed
Blessed be wheat from Germany and Sweden, for it will sprout in uncommon cold
Blessed be canola from Hungary, for it will warm us when the oil rigs drown
Blessed be fava from Italy, for it will hold down the soil after nuclear winds
Blessed be the kola nut from Nigeria, for it will keep our sentries awake
Blessed be damiana from Mexico, for it will coax the phallus from its sheath
Blessed be kava kava from Samoa, for it will bring us untroubled sleep
Blessed be lotus edulis from Algeria, for it will feed our hunger for beauty
Blessed be coriander from Egypt, for it will seed manna in the heavens
Blessed be seer's salvia from the Sierras, for it will dare us to dream again.

And dream they do, of their frozen Galatea, created with their own hands,
not of frantic mothers pacing streets for stolen girls,
not of phantom daughters Facebooked on hydro poles,
not of Eve's seeds—scattered, unplanted, unmade:

in the refuse pails of Punjabi midwives, her neck twisted once
in the dying rooms of a Chinese orphanage, caked in her own waste
in the garbage heaps of Islamabad, baby mouth sucking at the sky
in the scarlet stain at the Taiwan clinic, after the sonogram
in the mine fields of Vietnam, her brothers sent in her wake
in a Chilean child brothel, the Bolivian recruiter had lied
in split-level Philadelphia, tongue tied by her partner's rage
in a Mexican villa, night prey at drug-runner hazings
in stale rooms in Afghanistan, teenaged boy on guard outside
in the melted faces of Bangladeshi girls, who paid for their defiance
inert in the churn of Darfur sand, chased down in the militia strike
in a mass grave near a Serbian rape factory, breasts sliced away
in the airless heat of full-body hoods, to save others from desire
in the shroud of childbed sheets, sewn shut to keep her chaste
in pig-manure piles in Canada, a stray foot or hand or eye
in the annihilating blackness along the Highway of Tears
in the jewelled ashes of the bride-burning pyre.

Arleen Paré

DECEMBER 6, 1989

      ask yourself how you bear this state   everyday   this chromosomal state of x
plus x   like the day you step from the number seventeen   cross the street   up the concrete
steps   faster   along the corridor into the university classroom   late   and a boy
with a semi-automatic rushes in and starts shooting   starts shouting   a December
everyday   the sixth   says he hates women   says he hates feminists   he tells the
men in the classroom to leave and they do   and then he shoots round after round
until you are all shot   the x on your sweaters marks you   you bear this state of target
and in the news your mothers cry for you and your sisters cry and your aunts and
girlfriends cry   you are every woman in the city   this December everyday   the
hard-packed snow still moans beneath your everywoman boots as you hunch home
from your job as a nanny or your job in the greasy spoon dishing poutine and gravy
you ask yourself how you bear it

      you are every woman   you understand warnings by your parents   don't
take candy   don't expect too much   by your husband in the kitchen when you arrive
late with the kids from daycare and the groceries and set the bags on the counter and
he says see what happens   what did they expect

      how you bear it   ask yourself why   you are in all the cities   you are up
and down fence-bound laced-up country lanes   you are on windbeaten coastlines
in shiploads of refugees   in prisons   in bedrooms   on streets pacing for the next trick
you bear it   the state of want   the state of use   the state of disrespect of ridicule of
wishing you were dead ask yourself why   and if no good answer comes

      tear down every poster every newsstand every high-tension wire every
billboard every high-rise   every highway sign leading out of town   every aeroplane
in the sky   every high and mighty penthouse hotel every bar and grill   tear up every
alley where you were hurt every research paper that described you and got it wrong
every house that trapped you every letter every spite every thought that thought you
less every x and y with too much breath in your face or too much blade at your throat
every shout every temper every gust of grit around your feet every car parked outside
your door every doorway every bank every bonnet every promise every classroom
every boy with a semi-automatic under his right arm rushing in yelling freeze
just before you do

Contributors

Jancis M. Andrews was born in Northumbria, UK, in 1934. At fourteen, she ran away from her violent home and refused to return to school. On immigrating to Canada, she enrolled in Grade Nine correspondence courses, finally obtaining a BFA from UBC. An award-winning writer, she is the author of *Rapunzel, Rapunzel, Let Down Your Hair* (Ronsdale Press) and *Walking on Water* (Cormorant Books). She is now a community volunteer living in Sechelt, BC.

Trysh Ashby-Rolls writes on challenging social issues. She is the author of *Triumph: A Journey of Healing from Incest* (McGraw-Hill Ryerson), forthcoming in paperback from Phoenix Books, and *The Left-Behind Dad: A Father's Search for His Missing Children* (forthcoming). She holds an MA with Distinction in Women's Studies and Education.

Avra is a performance poet and writer. She hopes this book brings women together and enables those dealing with abuse to feel less isolated and alone.

Janet Baker recently completed her BFA with Distinction at the University of Victoria with a double major in Writing and History In Art. She paints and writes in Mississauga, Ontario; Victoria, British Columbia; or elsewhere.

Yvonne Blomer's first collection of poetry, *a broken mirror, fallen leaf,* was shortlisted for The Gerald Lampert Memorial Award in 2007. She has an MA from the University of East Anglia and her work has been published in the UK, Japan and Canada. Her poems have been widely anthologized and she has twice been shortlisted for the CBC Literary Awards. Poems in this anthology are from Yvonne's unpublished manuscript *Death of Persephone*; she would like to acknowledge the BC Arts Council for financial support to work on this manuscript.

Kate Braid has published five books of poetry and three books of non-fiction. Her poetry has been nominated for several prizes and has won the Pat Lowther Memorial Award and the Vancity Women's Book Prize. Before becoming a teacher of creative writing, she worked for fifteen years as a labourer, apprentice and journey carpenter in construction. "Framing Job" is an excerpt from her upcoming memoir, *Journeywoman*.

Susan Braley lives in Victoria, BC, where she writes full-time. Her fiction and poetry have appeared in various publications, including *The Harpweaver, Madwoman in the Academy, Island Writer, Canadian Woman Studies* and *Arc Poetry Magazine*. Her poem "Traces" won *Arc*'s 2010 Readers' Choice Award.

Ruth Carrier was brought up in Toronto, Ontario, during the Great Depression. She started working at age fourteen, and her father kept all her earnings until she left home at age twenty-one. She believes the school of hard knocks is not so bad if you keep your nose to the grindstone and try to stay positive. She turns eighty this year.

Bharat Chandramouli is a feminist, scientist, environmentalist and budding social-justice activist. He considers supporting his partner, a survivor of sexualized violence, through her difficult journey to be one of the most challenging experiences of his adult life, but would not have it any other way. He has always learned more from his mistakes than from his successes, so he urges people to put the interests of their survivor partner or friend above their own fears and insecurities.

Zhong M. Chen, winner of the First Prize for Best Essay in Chinese Canadian Literature, a Silver Prize and an Excellence Award in two international literary competitions, has had his work published in *Maple Family, New Voices: An Anthology of Post-1967 Chinese Canadian Writing in the Lower Mainland, Thursdays, Thursdays II, Thursdays III: These Words*. He has also authored an academic book, *The Influence of Daoism on Asian-Canadian Writers,* and a collection of poetry, prose and pictures, *Best of East and West,* funded by the City Hall of Vancouver. He has done readings of his works at the Carnegie Centre, the Brickhouse and the Rhizome Café.

Emma Cochrane grew up in Nova Scotia and La Paz, Bolivia. She has worked throughout British Columbia as a planting foreman and now lives in Victoria where she works in social services. Emma is one of the founders of *LoudSpeaker Festival,* a festival of music, theatre and poetry in celebration of International Women's Day. She has a BA in Women's Studies and Spanish from the University of Victoria.

Michelle Demers has been a carpenter for twenty-five years and continues to be a carpenter at age fifty-four. She lives with her dog and is currently working on home renovations. She has been clean and sober for twenty years.

Sonia Di Placido published her first chapbook of poems, *Vulva Magic* (LyricalMyracle Press), in 2004, and her second chapbook, *Forest Primitive* (Aeolus House Press), in 2008. She is currently completing a Master of Fine Art in Creative Writing through the University of British Columbia. Sonia lives in Toronto, Ontario.

Wendy Donawa spent most of her life in the Caribbean, and is now a semi-retired academic, poet and tai chi enthusiast on Vancouver Island. Her poems have appeared in Caribbean and Canadian literary journals, and she received the Victoria Writers Society first prize for poetry in their summer 2009 competition. Her chapbook, *Sliding Towards Equinox* (Rubicon Press), was published in 2009.

Leah Fowler is a professor in Education. She has worked as a postal clerk, waitress, house-painter, Canada Post sorter, driving instructor, firewood provider, recreation therapist for institutionalized children with severe challenges, bookstore clerk and research assistant in radiation genetics. As an old biologist, she likes to kayak and garden. Music, meditation, tai chi, art, literature, and gentle, sentient people contribute to her best consciousness.

David Fraser lives in Nanoose Bay, BC. He is the founder and editor of *Ascent Aspirations Magazine*, which debuted in 1997. His poetry and short fiction have appeared in several journals and anthologies, including *Rocksalt: An Anthology of Contemporary BC Poetry*. He is the author of three collections of poetry: *Going to the Well*, *Running Down the Wind* and *No Way Easy*. To keep out of trouble, he helps develop the spoken-word series WordStorm in Nanaimo, BC (www.wordstorm.ca).

Elee Kraljii Gardiner directs the Thursdays Writing and Editing Collectives in the Downtown Eastside of Vancouver, BC. She is the founder of Otter Press, the editor of four chapbook anthologies and leads workshops on creativity, writing and editing. Elee's writing has appeared in Canadian and US publications; Spanish translations of her work are forthcoming.

Jackie Gay was born in Birmingham, England, and now lives in Victoria, BC. She has published two novels, *Scapegrace* (Tindal Street Press) and *Wist* (Tindal Street Press), and edited three collections of short stories. Her short stories have been published in *London Magazine* and *The Malahat Review*.

Christin Geall has worked as a newspaper columnist, magazine editor and food writer, and in publicity with Beacon Press before completing the Stonecoast MFA in Creative Nonfiction. She now teaches in the Department of Writing at the University of Victoria.

Sara Graefe is an award-winning playwright and screenwriter. Her work has appeared in *Lady Driven, Hot & Bothered 4, With A Rough Tongue, Literary Mama* and on *The Memoir Blog*. She lives in Vancouver, BC, with her wife, young son and two black pugs.

Elizabeth Haynes's "The Alchemist," first appeared in *The Malahat Review*, no. 167. Her non-fiction piece "Seventeen Postcards," also set in Bolivia, was shortlisted for the James H. Gray Award for Short Nonfiction at the 2010 Alberta Literary Awards. Elizabeth has completed a novel, *The Errant Husband*, set in Canada and Cuba. Her short-story collection, *Speak Mandarin Not Dialect* (Thistledown Press) was a finalist for the 2000 Alberta Book Awards. She grew up in Kamloops, BC, and writes in Calgary, Alberta.

Anne Hopkinson lives in Burnaby and writes everywhere and anywhere she happens to be. She writes a monthly column for the *Burnaby NewsLeader*. Anne also writes with the Thursdays Writing Collective at the Carnegie Centre in downtown Vancouver, BC. She is an alumni of the SFU Writers Studio.

Auto Jansz is a folk musician. She lives and works in Victoria, BC.

Harvey Jenkins lives in Nanaimo, BC. His poems have been published in the *Western Producer, Manitoba Myriad: An Anthology of Poetry and Prose* and *Ascent Aspirations Magazine*. In the fall of 2009, four of his poems were anthologized in *One Sweet Ride: An Easy Writers' Anthology* (Ascent Aspirations Publishing).

Fazeela Jiwa left teaching in the public school system for direct action with a feminist rape crisis centre and transition house in Vancouver, BC. She is pursuing graduate work at Concordia University, using fiction and poetry as media that transform social structures.

Ruth Johnston grew up in Prince George, BC, and received her Bachelor of Arts (Honours) from the University of Victoria. She is currently working on her first collection of poems.

Fiona Tinwei Lam is a Scottish-born, Vancouver-based writer whose work has appeared in literary magazines across Canada, as well as in over fourteen anthologies. Her book of poetry, *Intimate Distances,* (Nightwood Editions) was a finalist for the City of Vancouver Book Award. Her latest collection of poetry is *Enter the Chrysanthemum* (Caitlin Press). More information about Fiona can be found on fionalam.net.

Born in the south of England, **Joanna Lilley** has always strived to go north, which is why in 1991 she cycled almost ten thousand kilometres across Canada from Halifax, Nova Scotia, to Inuvik, Northwest Territories. It took her another fifteen years to move permanently to Canada, leaving behind her family but bringing her cat. Joanna now lives in Whitehorse, Yukon, where she writes poems and stories. Her work has been published in journals and anthologies such as *Rogue Stimulus* (Mansfield Press), *Arctica* and *The Northern Review.*

Maeengan Linklater is a First Nations writer and filmmaker. His first film, *Winnipeg First Nation: The Heart of a Home,* co-produced with Jim Sanderson, premiered at Cinematheque in Winnipeg in 2009. He has published two poetry chapbooks with the Aboriginal Writers Collective of Manitoba. Maeengan serves the board of the Manitoba Writers Guild and is a member of the Aboriginal Writers Collective of Manitoba.

Christine Lowther is the author of the poetry books *My Nature* and *New Power,* and the co-author and co-editor of *Writing the West Coast: In Love with Place*, a collection of non-fiction nature writing and memoir. She lives on the west coast of Vancouver Island.

Brittany Luby is a non-status Anishinaabe author from Kenora, Ontario. She has a BAH in English from Queen's University and an MA in history from York University. She is now completing her doctorate in History at the University of British Columbia. Most recently, her work was published in *Red Ink Magazine* and *Native Literatures Generations.*

Sheila Martindale came to Victoria, BC, in 2009, after living in England; Montreal; London, Ontario; and Calgary. She is the author of eight books of poetry; the next is due to be published in fall 2010. She is currently the poetry editor of *Island Writer* magazine.

Rhona McAdam returned to live in Victoria, BC, in 2002, after living in London, England, for twelve years. In 2007 she spent a year studying at Slow Food's University of Gastronomic Sciences in Italy. She has published five books of poetry. Her most recent is *Cartography* (Oolichan Books). Rhona's poems in this anthology are from her unpublished manuscript, *The Earth's Kitchen*.

Jessica Michalofsky parents, teaches and writes in Victoria, BC. Her work has been published in chapbooks and in journals such as *Event, CV2* and *The Malahat Review*. She's wild about syntax and grammar and punctuation and urges you to consider grammar as a site of radical expression.

Of **Susan Musgrave** a Toronto bookseller wrote, "I've discovered the ultimate combination of books for Anarchist Grade Nine (to 12) girls: *The Story of O* by Pauline Réage and *Things That Keep and Do Not Change* by Musgrave. If someone offered those two books as a package deal to angry young femmes I think Susan would become rich off poetry royalties." Susan's all-time favourite review of her poetry came from a high-school student after she gave a reading of her work: "Susan Musgrave has made me hate poetry a little less." Susan Musgrave lives on Haida Gwaii, where she has recently become the owner of Copper Beech House Inn.

Madeleine Nattrass has been published in *Quills Canadian Poetry Magazine, Tower Poetry, Other Voices, filling Station, FreeFall Magazine, Women and Environments International, The New Quarterly* and *CV2*. Born in Alberta, she is a retired French immersion teacher, now living on Vancouver Island. She is very pleased to be participating in this effort to end violence against women.

Arleen Paré is a Victoria poet and writer. Her first mixed-genre novel, *Paper Trail*, was nominated for the Dorothy Livesay Poetry Prize in 2008 and won the Victoria Butler Book Prize in the same year. She is a graduate student in University of Victoria's Creative Writing program.

Kelly Pitman is originally from Alberta. She teaches English at Camosun College in Victoria, BC, and reads whenever and wherever she can.

Roy Roberts is a Vancouver, BC, poet living at the ARC (Artist Resource Centre) with his wife, ceramic artist Shelley Holmes, and his son, painter Jordan Roberts. His poetry has appeared in *Prairie Fire* and three other anthologies.

Janet Marie Rogers is a West Coast Mohawk writer, spoken-word artist and radio host living on un-surrendered Coast Salish territory. Her video poem, "What Did You Do Boy," and second spoken-word CD, *Firewater*, featuring five native musicians, was released in 2009. She is the host of CFUV's *Native Waves Radio* and a music columnist on CBC's *All Points West*.

Caitlin Ross has spent twenty-one years cultivating a taste for small pleasures, and maintaining a revolving door of grand ideas and secret dreams.

Andrea Routley is the co-founder and coordinator of the *LoudSpeaker Festival* in Victoria, BC. She grew up in British Columbia's Fraser Valley, moved several times, taught preschool, ESL and has planted lots of trees. She attended Camosun College's Creative Writing program and is currently completing her degree at the University of Victoria.

Dawn Service sometimes lives in an old log cabin she restored on the shores of Anahim Lake in the west Chilcotin area of British Columbia. Her piece, "The Village Idiot," is an excerpt from a manuscript called *Wilderness Bliss*.

Janet K. Smith has been happily married for sixteen years. Her family includes three dogs and two cats. She is an avid reader, golfer, home renovator, dog trainer and Burning Man participant. She is fascinated by the resilience of the human spirit, and the role of emotions in defining character as well as an individual's perception of reality.

Madeline Sonik is a writer and anthologist whose fiction, poetry and creative non-fiction have appeared in literary journals internationally. Her novel, *Arms*, and her collection of short fiction, *Drying the Bones*, were published by Nightwood Editions. She is also the author of a children's novel, *Belinda and the Dustbunnys* (Hodgepog Books) and a poetry collection, *Stone Sightings* (Inanna Publications). She teaches creative writing at the University of Victoria.

Yasuko Thanh has been published in various literary magazines including *Descant*, *Fiddlehead* and *Prairie Fire*. Her non-fiction has appeared in publications such as the *Vancouver Review* and *subTerrain*. In 2009, she won the Journey Prize for short fiction. Her first book, a collection of stories, is forthcoming from McClelland & Stewart in 2011.

Mildred Tremblay lives in Nanaimo, BC. She has two books of poetry and one book of short stories published by Oolichan Books. Her latest book of poems is *The Thing About Dying* (Oolichan Books). Mildred has won many awards for her work, and has been published widely in literary magazines and anthologies. Most recently, she was nominated Poet of the Year by Passager Books at the University of Baltimore.

Andrew Wade is a young actor and writer finishing up a concurrent BFA and BA degrees at the University of Victoria. One recent acting highlight was playing Iago in a Big Ideas/Victoria Shakespeare Society production of *Othello, The Moor of Venice* (2010). His plays have recently been performed by Vancouver's IGNITE! Festival, SATCo Theatre and the University of Victoria's Studio Series. He loves superheroes, working with children and encouraging curiosity and learning. Online, Andrew can be found at adewade.wordpress.com and andrewwade.net.

Nasstasia Yard is a singer-songwriter and poet living in Vancouver, BC. Her music can be heard at myspace.com/nasstasiayard. She is currently working on releasing her first album.

Algebra Young is from Victoria, BC. Having struggled with dyslexia since early childhood, she has worked hard to overcome her obstacles and graduated from Victoria High School with honours. She attends Camosun College when she is not out exploring the world or on wacky adventures.